F

TI

Timepieces is a cycle
Suffolk village. Follow
story for every month in the year, reflecting the
different seasons and relationships which occur in
Brayford. There is the story of a race between two
boys to find a missing tortoise. There is a story about a
family's stay in a beautiful country house, when they
discover it is not the paradise they had expected.
There are stories about conker fights and bullies, the
death of a family pet and a disastrous school trip. A
strong sense of a passing year emerges, during which
the reader is given a delightful insight into the dramas
enacted by the various children and their families.

David Leney has been a primary school teacher since
1971. He began writing stories for children some
years ago, reading them to the classes he taught. He is
now head teacher of a primary school in a village near
Ipswich, and lives in the seaside town of Felixstowe.

Also by David Leney

THE LANDFILL

· TIMEPIECES ·

David Leney

Illustrated by Anthony Kerins

PUFFIN BOOKS

FOR MY MOTHER

PUFFIN BOOKS

Published by the Penguin Group
Penguin Books Ltd, 27 Wrights Lane, London W8 5TZ, England
Viking Penguin, a division of Penguin Books USA Inc.
375 Hudson Street, New York, New York 10014, USA
Penguin Books Australia Ltd, Ringwood, Victoria, Australia
Penguin Books Canada Ltd, 2801 John Street, Markham, Ontario, Canada L3R 1B4
Penguin Books (NZ) Ltd, 182–190 Wairau Road, Auckland 10, New Zealand

Penguin Books Ltd, Registered Offices: Harmondsworth, Middlesex, England

First published by J. M. Dent & Sons Ltd, 1989
Published in Puffin Books 1990
1 3 5 7 9 10 8 6 4 2

Text copyright © David Leney, 1989
Illustrations copyright © Anthony Kerins, 1989
All rights reserved

Printed and bound in Great Britain by
Cox & Wyman Ltd, Reading, Berks.

Contents

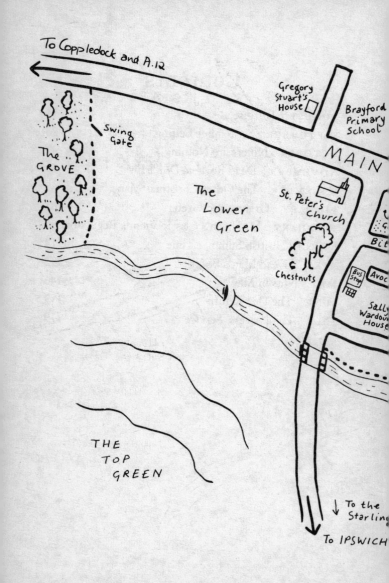

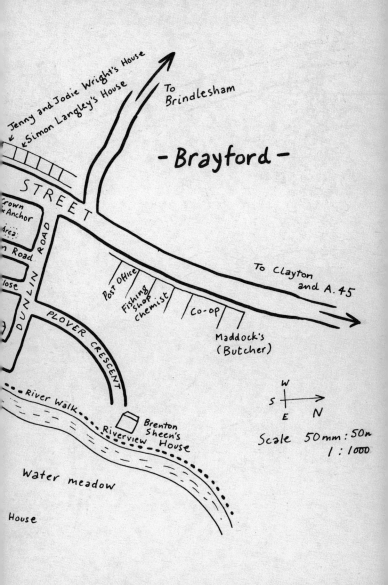

Jenny and Jodie Wright's House

Simon Langley's House

To Brindlesham

- Brayford -

STREET

Crown & Anchor

Area:
Road

Close

DUNDON ROAD

PLOVER CRESCENT

Post Office

Fishing Shop

Chemist

Co-op

Maddock's
(Butcher)

To Clayton
and A.45

River Walk

Brenton
Sheen's
House

Riverview

Water meadow

House

W
S — N
E

Scale 50mm : 50m
1 : 1000

Tortoise

'What are you staring at?' Brenton Sheen demanded, as if it were a crime for anybody else to look at the small ads in the window of Brayford Post Office.

Simon glanced round at the tall boy with his sleek, dark hair and even darker eyes.

'Nothing in particular,' he muttered.

Although he went to the same school as Brenton and was even in the same class, he hardly knew him. They only lived five minutes apart – Brenton in the most expensive house on the most expensive end of the most expensive estate; Simon in a terraced house on Main Street. Blond, slow and fat, he could never begin to keep up with Brenton, and he knew it. Brenton talked faster, walked faster, rode his bike further, jumped higher and spelt better. Brenton had learnt all his tables by the time he was seven. Brenton's dad had seen to that.

'Go on! What are you gawping at?'

'Nothing much.'

'More fool you! Most of those ads are out of date anyway.'

Simon Langley was not cunning. He sometimes tried to be, but never quite succeeded. Perhaps he didn't really want to be cunning. Maybe that was the problem. He stopped staring at PRAM FOR SALE and moved over to SECONDHAND TYPEWRITER VERY GOOD CONDITION. But he knew it was no use. In seconds Brenton had checked every card.

11

'No, you don't want a pram or a typewriter. But I bet I know what you do want! Simple Simon wants ten pounds!'

Simon winced. It was no good pretending. Brenton had understood everything.

'Simple Simon wants the ten-pound reward,' he repeated. He then read out the card:

LOST
INDIAN STARRED TORTOISE
APPROX 10 INCHES LONG
MATURE MALE
If found, please return to
11 AVOCET CLOSE
TEN POUND REWARD

'People are stupid,' Brenton said.

'How come?'

'Well, if they didn't want to lose the tortoise, they should have drilled a hole in the edge of its shell at the back, tied on a piece of string and tethered it to a stake. My uncle had a tortoise and that's what he did.'

'Really? How old is it now?'

'It isn't old.'

'How do you mean?'

'It's dead. Anyway, it was only an animal.'

So that was it! A tortoise was *only* an animal. Maybe the lost tortoise meant a lot to someone, but to Brenton it was just a shell that happened to cover a lump of flesh. It was worth exactly ten pounds – no more, no less.

'You can go and look at secondhand prams if you like,' said Brenton, 'but I'm going to get that tortoise.'

'Maybe we could both ...'

'*What?* We could both *what?*'

'Maybe we could both look. We'd have a much better chance of finding it if we both ...'

'Oh yeah! And what do we do with the ten-pound note? Don't tell me you want to split it!'

'I'm not too bothered about ...'

'All right, Saint Simon! All right, Saint Simple Simon! Maybe you won't admit it, but I bet you want that ten-pound note as much as I do. So I'll tell you what we'll do. You go your way, I'll go mine. Whoever finds the tortoise gets the reward. Not half the reward – all of it!'

Before Simon could agree or disagree, Brenton had gone.

They met up again twenty minutes later, outside a bungalow – 11 Avocet Close. Simon had only just found it. Brenton had already been inside, talked to the owners and jotted down some details about the lost tortoise. Simon did not feel he could go inside as well – the people would not want to be disturbed all over again.

'What did they tell you?' he asked Brenton.

Brenton said that if he needed the information so badly, then he should have got there first.

As both boys had to go home for lunch, the tortoise hunt did not start properly till early that afternoon. Simon knew he would have to begin in the area around Avocet Close. At two-thirty, he tried number 13 – the bungalow next to the owners.

'Your friend already asked. Why don't you ask him?' an elderly woman suggested. The door closed again before Simon could explain.

The bungalow on the other side – number 10 – was empty. At least, nobody answered the doorbell. Perhaps they were away on holiday. Simon wondered if it would be safe to search the garden. Then a dog started to bark and pound against the fence. He decided it was best to move on.

What was needed was a plan. If the tortoise had crawled out of the close, then he would have to try every house on the estate, no matter how long it took or how much he hated asking. Bittern Road was next. He tried number 1.

'No, I have not seen a tortoise,' a man in pyjamas yawned. 'I work nights and I'm meant to sleep days. That's twice I've been woken up in one afternoon!'

'Twice?' Simon enquired.

'Yes. Once by one of your mates – and now by you!'

'Sorry.'

'*You're* sorry! How do you think *I* feel?'

Half-heartedly, Simon searched the grass area behind the Crown and Anchor. What was the point? It was like looking for a needle in a haystack. Maybe the tortoise could have cut through the alley to Main Street. But there wasn't much point in following that up until he'd searched the Gippen Estate properly.

It began to drizzle. Simon, in an old sweater but with no coat, walked back towards the bungalow and tried one last door.

'You expect me to sponsor you?' a woman asked. 'Do you realize I been asked to sponsor three lots in the last month? Sponsored spell-in at the Primary School – we got to pay children to spell these days? Sponsored knit-in – I ask you! – at the Brownies. Sponsored swim by the Boy's Brigade. I know their game! Five p a length and they wad 'em up so they wouldn't sink if you dropped 'em in the middle of the North Sea. Next thing you know, you owe 'em a fortune. No thank you! Politeness! That's what I say. They ought to sponsor a little bit of politeness!'

Simon realized he had wasted all Monday afternoon. If he carried on like this, he'd waste half his summer holiday.

On Tuesday morning he was out of the house by nine

o'clock. The weather was clearer and he didn't bother with a coat.

He had intended to walk along Main Street till he reached the zebra crossing by the Co-op. But fifty yards earlier he caught sight of Brenton's racing bike, balanced on its stand just outside the Post Office. Even before he reached the other pavement, he was aware of a gap in the top right-hand corner of the small ads board. It made him feel sick. He wanted to sit down. He wanted to sit down because life wasn't very fair. Just as he feared, the postcard had been taken from the window. That meant the tortoise must have been found by someone. Again he glanced at Brenton's bike, parked outside.

He shuffled into the Post Office and stood behind a magazine rack. From there he could see Brenton at the counter.

'That's it, Mrs Trinder. Mr Hill told me to tell you to take the card down. No point in people looking for an animal that's already been found.'

Simon's throat began to ache. He swallowed, but the lump of pain seemed to be stuck.

'Oh, do you happen to sell maps?'

'Would that be a map of Suffolk you want?' asked Mrs Trinder, in her slow, dry voice. She sounded tired. Since her husband was ill, she was having to cope alone.

'No. A map of the village.'

The lump still stuck in Simon's throat, but his eyes lit up.

'Well, there is a map – just a hand-drawn thing that the Parish Council do. You want one of them? Five p.'

Brenton bought it. Simon watched him slip the sheet into a plastic envelope which he then attached to a clip-board. He stared at the map for a few seconds, then suddenly left the shop. Simon could see him out on the pavement, grabbing his bike and pushing the stand up with his foot. He held the clipboard in his right hand and with his other hand steered the bike.

So, the hunt was still on! Simon would have bought a map as well, but he'd forgotten to bring any money with him. He left the shop and turned into Dunlin Road. No doubt about it, he would have to toughen up. Whether he wanted to or not, he had to go to 11 Avocet Close and talk to Mr Hill for himself.

As Brenton hared round the streets of Brayford on his racer, Simon shuffled reluctantly towards the bungalow. He made his way up the garden path with the slow, laboured movement of an elderly tortoise. He put a finger on to the doorbell, closed his eyes and pushed.

'Yes, you've got the right bungalow,' said Mrs Hill. 'Your friend came here yesterday afternoon. Come in – but mind Ben. We have to keep him in, as he's had a nasty summer cold. Don't worry – just step over him.'

'Bet you didn't know that!' a deep voice boomed. 'Bet you didn't know that the tortoise can catch a cold, the same as you or me!'

'That's it,' repeated Mrs Hill. 'Just step over him.'

Simon did as he was told and entered an L-shaped living room. He narrowly avoided stepping on a second tortoise.

'Do you like Battenberg?'

He bent down to look more closely. The tortoise gave

16

out a tiny hiss and pulled in his head and limbs.

'Yes. I think he's very ... very nice.'

Simon was not too sure how you paid compliments to a tortoise.

'No, dear. The tortoise is called Molly. Battenberg is a sort of cake with almond icing. Would you like a piece?'

Simon smiled nervously and nodded. The second tortoise, Molly, suddenly burst into action, covering three yards in about half a minute. Simon followed it as it turned left into the other section of the room. A tall man, wearing a dressing-gown over his shirt and tie, lay on the sofa. He looked grey and tired, but smiled in Simon's direction.

'Yes,' he boomed. 'This is Molly, Ben's wife. Nothing wrong with you, old girl. Nothing wrong with you, my little testudo!'

'I thought you said her name was Molly,' Simon muttered nervously.

'And so it is. "Testudo" is simply the Latin word for a tortoise.'

Mrs Hill arrived with a slice of window-cake on a plate.

'Don't worry too much about him,' she whispered. 'He doesn't normally talk like an encyclopedia. It's his nerves, you see. It's worry. He's going into hospital this afternoon for a gallstone operation. On top of all that, there's Thomas gone missing. Thomas – the first tortoise we ever had! Twenty-two years old. No wonder John's in a bit of a state!'

'He could easily survive on wild plants, grubs and so on,' Mr Hill suddenly blurted out. 'But there's roads to worry about – and garden machinery like rotary mowers.' As he spoke, he had risen shakily to his feet and now stared at Simon as if pleading for help. Molly, curving her four paws beneath her shell, suddenly extended her neck.

17

Pushing with all her force, she lifted her whole body upward by an inch or more.

'Now she's showing off,' said Mrs Hill. 'She knows we're worried about Thomas. Jealousy, that is! She's just playing for attention. Would you like to pick her up? . . . Sorry, I don't remember your name.'

'Simon,' the boy said, bending down. He did not think a tortoise had teeth, but Molly's jaws looked hard and horny. He put his hands out cautiously and lifted her from the carpet. The weight of the tortoise – the solid feel and the unexpected warmth – transmitted themselves through his hands and into his whole body. He turned away and, pretending to look at the garden, closed his eyes. All that he expected and feared – the coldness of the shell, the naked underbelly, the nip and stench of head and tail – all this had gone.

'Carapace and plastron – upper shell and lower,' intoned Mr Hill. 'These live and grow, live and grow. People do not understand. They paint them and drill holes through them. In the case of the poor turtle, they even kill the creatures and carve their shells into ornaments and trinkets. People, you see, are cruel through ignorance.'

Simon turned and looked at the tall, bald man. He seemed grey and sad.

Molly suddenly poked out her head. A hind leg brushed the inside of Simon's wrist; he felt the scratch of a tiny claw.

'Just look at them!' Mrs Hill laughed. He realized she was staring over his shoulder, through the window, on to the lawn. Startled, he saw them too, all over the garden: tortoises levering themselves about or lying docile in the sun. Shells marked out in ebony and ochre, ringed in green as deep as shadowed leaves, or patterned with delicate bursts of pale yellow stars. It seemed to Simon that here, on the Gippen Estate in the village of Brayford, the life of an ancient wilderness suddenly crawled everywhere. Amongst it he spotted the claws of lizards and the hinged jaws of the serpent. Dragon scales too – and the folded skins of minute dinosaurs. Front limbs tested blades of grass with the strength to move boulders. Rear limbs scudded, as reptiles laboured through another inch of time.

Quite close to him, a tortoise had managed to prop itself against a low wall. It tilted like a dinner plate on the shelf of a dresser.

'That's Victor. He does that to catch the sun. Sun is vital to the health of the shell,' explained Mr Hill.

Then it was feeding time and Mrs Hill took Simon outside. He waited a moment while she went to fetch a bucket of chopped vegetables from the kitchen. Mr Hill waved weakly through the window, then went back to the sofa, to sleep again.

After Simon had helped with the feeding, he knew it was time to be going.

He didn't see Brenton again till Friday afternoon. Simon had just finished checking the verges of a path that led from the Warders' house to the Ipswich Road.

'Waste of time looking there,' Brenton sniggered. 'I already searched every inch of it.'

He sat astride his racer. The map was now fixed in front of him by a special holder that clipped on to the handlebars.

'I can tell you, there are 147 houses on this estate, and I've made a list of them, and I've been to every one of them. This afternoon I'm going to do the other side of Main Street. You'll see! I'll get him in the end.'

'Good luck, then!' Simon mumbled.

'I don't need luck. I got a system.'

19

Simon had no system. He spent the early afternoon wandering about in the hot sunshine looking everywhere and nowhere. By three o'clock he'd had enough. He crossed the Ipswich Road and lay down on the warm grass between the conker trees and the churchyard on the Lower Green. For half an hour he dozed off. He was annoyed to be woken up by several young children. The Wright twins, who never stopped talking, had always annoyed him.

'You want one, then?' Jenny asked.

'Yip. I reckon,' Jodie answered.

At first Simon thought they were talking about sweets.

'You can't get 'em nowadays. That's against the law. They can't bring 'em into the country. That's what Dad say when I asked him.'

'Well, then,' Jodie demanded, 'how did Rebecca get one? She got a tortoise at home.'

Simon opened one eye. He sat up. Then he pumped them with questions.

'So Rebecca Starling's got a tortoise, has she?'

Jenny said, 'Yip.'

'And did she buy it?'

'Nope. That just walked into their garden.'

Simon had never moved so fast in his life. Within ten

minutes he had crossed the bridge and sweated up the Ipswich Road to the isolated house that stood between village and town. He crept round the side and peered over the fence. He could not see the tortoise, but only a wooden box and a run made of chicken wire, right in the middle of the lawn.

A girl, freckled and redheaded, knelt in the run itself. He knew Rebecca Starling. She was at his school, in the Infants.

Then his heart sank. He had won! He had only to wait around a bit, nip through the gate and lift out Thomas. But already he thought of Rebecca in tears. He felt slow and fat again. The truth was, he was not made for winning.

As the girl broke lettuce leaves for her pet, Simon shuffled off towards home.

It was one of the worst nights he could remember. Every ten or fifteen minutes he seemed to wake up. He must have rolled over a hundred times. Sometimes, as he tossed and turned, he would think of Mr Hill in his hospital bed. Maybe they had already done the operation. Maybe he had spent the night in some pain. Maybe *he* was thinking of the grand old tortoise – now lost or dead.

Then Simon would roll over again and think of the thin, freckled girl. She couldn't have been more than four or five. That was about a quarter of the tortoise's age. She had looked after him for hardly a week. Was that it? Was she really going to lose him?

At other moments he found himself thinking about Brenton. Brenton had a fast bike, a map and a system. Perhaps the Starlings' house was too far out of the village to be marked on the map. But it wouldn't make much difference in the end. In the end, Brenton might also overhear conversations. 'I'll get that tortoise! You'll see!' It was only a question of time.

Just before dawn broke, his baby sister started crying. Normally he would have pulled the blankets over his head and slept on while Emily was given her first feed. Not today. His mother was amazed when, just as she'd warmed up the milk, Simon suddenly clomped into the kitchen, untidy but fully dressed.

'What on earth's got into you?' she asked. 'Since you're up, you can feed Emily.'

Mechanically he pushed the teat into the tiny mouth. As Emily gurgled, Mrs Langley drank a coffee and stared at her son. He was amazing. For weeks on end he'd lounge about. Then, without warning, he would suddenly burst into life. She did not know whether to be pleased or annoyed. By seven o'clock he had done his own breakfast and left the house.

'See you later,' he said. His voice was quite sharp. It was all very odd – as if he'd actually decided to do something.

By seven-fifteen he stood panting by the fence of the Starlings' garden. It didn't need much effort. Now that he knew what had to be done, doing it was no problem. 'Maybe I'm hardening up,' Simon thought, as he pushed his way through the side gate.

He stepped over the chicken wire, reached into the wooden shelter and, holding Thomas in both hands, marched out of the garden. He marched on down the hill till he'd crossed the bridge, then turned off the road to follow the River Walk. Passing the Warders' house, he turned left into Dunlin Road and before long he had reached the Hills' bungalow. All the curtains were still drawn in Avocet Close.

'Isn't it a bit early?' Mrs Hill asked. 'Oh, heavens! You found Thomas! The scallywag! Yes, that's him!'

22

She lunged at Simon and, just for a moment, he thought he was going to be kissed. But it was all right. She took the heavy reptile out of his hands and kissed the shell instead. Thomas stuck his head right out and twisted it upward as though he wanted to kiss her back, if she'd let him. She did. He nibbled her nose.

'Oh, Thomas!' a bass voice suddenly called. 'I thought you were gone for good!'

Simon spun round to see Mr Hill in his dressing-gown, standing by the doorway.

'But I thought you'd gone to hospital!'

'I did – and I'm home again!'

'But I thought they had to take out some stones.'

'That's right. Gallstones. But they decided to use micro-surgery. Put me to sleep, but never opened me up. They do it all with tiny cameras and miniature instruments on the end of tubes. The gallstones are gone and I feel fine.'

All the same, he had to sit down. Thomas crawled over the carpet towards him.

'We can't thank you enough,' said Mr Hill. 'You don't know how much it means to us!'

Simon thought he saw tears in his eyes. But this was no time to go soft.

'I wonder . . .'

'Yes?'

'Well, in the advert you said that . . .'

'Sorry?'

'You said something about a reward. I think you mentioned ten pounds.'

'Of course!' Mrs Hill muttered. 'Of course! I'll fetch it for you now.' She sounded surprised – and disappointed. They'd have paid him without his insisting.

'No thank you,' Simon said.

Mrs Hill stopped dead.

'I don't really want the ten pounds.'

'Well, why did you ask?'

'I want ... a small tortoise.'

The woman and her husband looked at each other; then back to the large, untidy boy.

'Do you promise ...'

'Oh yes. It'll be well looked after.'

'And you're sure you don't want the ten pounds?'

Simon shook his head. Mr Hill stood up slowly and edged his way, with some strain, to his wife's side. He spoke to her in a whisper, then smiled again at Simon.

'You may have an Indian starred tortoise, Simon. But only if you take this book as well.'

He took a copy from a drawer and, while Mrs Hill went out to the garden, placed it in the boy's hands.

One Saturday, in the middle of August, in a garden just outside the village of Brayford, a five-year-old girl knelt over a wooden box. From it she lifted an Indian starred tortoise – so young that its shell measured little more than four inches from head to tail.

One hand beneath it, one upon the top, she rose to her feet, turned and held the creature out towards her father.

'You see, Daddy! I told you. He's shrunk. He's really shrunk!'

The father bent down to look closer. With a tiny hiss, the reptile pulled its head back under cover.

'Don't be silly!' the man said quietly. 'Tortoises don't shrink!'

One week earlier a far larger tortoise had crawled into their garden. They had kept it, fed it with vegetable cuttings and, together, built a wooden shelter. Now it had disappeared and, in its place, there was a four-inch youngster. On its tiny, rounded shell a star pattern burst – the colour of dry sand.

'It's shrunk, Dad!' the girl insisted. '*And* it's changed colour!'

The man, as puzzled as his daughter, saw a book on the roof of the shelter. He read out the title:

Caring For Your Tortoise
A Simple Guide by J.R. and F.B. Hill

Still puzzled, he noticed that a piece of paper had been neatly folded and placed inside the front cover. He unfolded it and read it slowly. Rebecca did not miss a word.

This is a grandson of Thomas the First.
Please look after him.
By the way, Thomas the Second is what
you ought to call him.

Back at home, Simon lay on his bed. He felt he had earned a good long rest. He'd let Brenton carry on looking.

September Letting

'Don't gawp!' Mrs Langley said to her son, Simon. 'Don't just stand there gawping! Why can't you help unload the car? Do some work, like the rest of us!'

Simon couldn't understand the point of all the rush. A minute or two to take stock of the house and garden – just a minute or two – was not much to ask. 'After all,' he mused, 'we're going to spend a week here. It'd be nice to know what we've let ourselves in for before we settle in. Anyhow, if you can't gawp in the last week of the summer holidays, when can you gawp?'

As he stood by the car, peering at the end of the cottage, he felt as if his family had just floated into a kind of paradise. To the left of the drive stood an enormous copper beech. Beyond it, at the back of the cottage itself, untrimmed lawn slid downward. Forty or fifty feet away it was broken up by vegetable patches, runner-bean supports, soft-fruit bushes and an old pear tree. Then the ground rose again and the garden ended in a steep bank, crowned with hazel and elder.

Mr Langley passed close to Simon, opened the back door of the car and, grunting, lifted out the carrycot. Inside it, little Emily was still sleeping. Mr Langley said, 'Mind out!' and bumped a corner of the carrycot against Simon's thigh. They couldn't wait a minute, could they!

Mr Langley struggled up to the main door with the cot. As he passed out of view, Simon took another minute to examine the front of the cottage. He liked the way the

26

drive bulged out into a large semi-circle – room enough for a car to turn in one. It was edged with a brick wall, old and moss-mottled. The mortar had long since crumbled away. It was hard to tell if the bricks were being held together or pushed apart by the force of roots and creepers. Above the wall, more lawn sloped upward. There were borders and circular flower beds, trellised roses and tubs everywhere.

Beyond it – countryside. No street. No pub. No shop. No housing estates. Just open countryside. Even the small town of Diss was four or five miles away. All his life, Simon had thought his home village, Brayford, was countryside. Well, it wasn't. As from this moment, it wasn't. Brayford might have been countryside once, but now it was almost part of Ipswich. Five years ago they'd started the Gippen Estate. Last year they'd built a second supermarket. Even the village high street was choked with evening traffic. Late into the night lorries rumbled by and shook the foundations of their terraced house. Maybe they'd build the bypass one day. But that would get rid of fields as well as lorries. Brayford was speeding up too much. Brayford wasn't countryside – not like this place.

Suddenly Simon realized he was holding a box of disposable nappies.

'Don't dawdle,' his father said. 'Go on. Take them inside.'

Stepping through the front door, he found himself in the kitchen. His mother was measuring powdered milk into a bottle. She filled it from the kettle, then held it under the cold tap to cool the mixture down.

'Here's the bottle and there's Emily,' she said. 'It's still too hot, but you take over.'

Simon didn't mind. He was good with the baby. Feeding Emily didn't bother him at all – it was one of the few jobs you could do while still sitting down. The slower the better. Thinking time. He tested the milk with a squirt against his left wrist, took Emily from her carrycot and settled down on a kitchen chair. Mrs Langley sat down too and smiled at her son.

Before Emily had half-finished the milk, Simon and his mother were surprised to see Mr Langley walking up the back garden. Somewhere he had found a clothcap. He also held a long stick, such as a farmer might use for driving sheep or cattle. His thumb in the V at the top, he swung it ahead with each step, till he stood just outside the window.

'Morning, Ma'am – and welcome to the estate.'

He touched the peak of the cap and grinned.

'Morning, Squire!' answered Mrs Langley.

'Do you be doing a little lunch for the squire?' her husband then enquired.

'Yes. But what exactly do you be doing?'

'I be picking a few pears for afters.'

'Barry!' she objected – her voice had shifted back to normal – 'You can't pick those pears. They're not ours!'

'Now do you listen here, my good wife! Either I do be

28

picking these pears or they do be rotting on the ground!'

Mrs Langley laughed and gave up.

Before Emily's feed was over, their father was back at the kitchen window. He peered in and placed four large, yellow pears on the sill. He had also put a red rose in the top buttonhole of his shirt. Then he was off again. Simon's mother took Emily and strapped her into the baby-bouncer.

'He could have brought a rose for me!' she giggled.

A minute later, the roar of an engine surprised them.

'What on earth . . .'

The noise seemed to come from the side of the house, but was moving up the drive. Louder. Deafening, now. Mr Langley's face passed across the front window. It swerved away. Mother and son gasped as they saw him wheeling round the drive on a tiny tractor, spluttering engine fumes into the fresh September air.

'What on earth's got into him?' Mrs Langley repeated. She sounded cross, but Simon noticed her muffling a giggle.

'Why, that be a grand morning!' They could only just hear his shout above the engine. 'We plough the fields and scatter . . .' he sang.

And Mr Langley was scattering all right. Beneath him the mower blades were down, gouging great whelks into the driveway and flinging up pebbles behind him.

'Barry! Barry! The blades are down!' Mrs Langley tried to tell him.

Mr Langley was still singing. He wrenched at the steering wheel, and the tractor – dwarfed beneath the bulk of the man – veered round the wall and up a bank and on to the top lawn. As it cut a diagonal strip across it, Mrs Langley ran behind. Suddenly the engine cut out. A final clank – and the blades stopped.

Simon, still in the kitchen, heard the baby behind him. Little snorts and suckings as she tried to find her thumb. He moved to the doorway and reached it just in time to see his father stepping off the mower. He threw the clothcap on to the ground and scratched his bald head.

'What got into you, Barry?'

He did not reply, but just stared at the strip of cut lawn.

'Just look at the drive, Barry! You know Mr Brant is coming this afternoon to collect our payment and show us round!'

Mr Langley thought a bit more.

'I had no idea the blades were down,' he said.

'Well, they were. It's too late now!'

'I'll... I'll... Well, I'll get the tractor going again and mow the lawn properly.'

'You can't leave it like that. That's for sure. I just hope you *can* get it going!'

'Of course I can. It only stopped because the fuel supply's off. Pipe's run dry. That's all. Just a question of finding the switch. All these engines are basically the same.'

Luckily Emily had found her thumb. No snorts now – only sucking. Simon left the doorway and walked over to the machine. By now his father had lifted back the cover and was poking about in the engine.

'Can I help?' Simon asked him.

'Is *this* it?' said his mother.

Fifteen minutes later the machine still stood at the end of the cut. Mrs Langley suggested they try pushing it back to the garage.

To Simon's surprise, his father just chortled. An odd, arrogant sound that Simon had not heard before. Then his mother laughed lazily. Something was coming over her too. She picked the clothcap off the grass and put it on her husband's head.

'It's not every week we're on holiday, Barry. Come on, let's have some lunch!'

All three of them ambled back to the kitchen. At last Simon's parents were relaxing.

If anybody felt tense now, it was the boy himself. He paused, allowing his mother and father to pass through the door before him.

They swaggered in as if... that was it!... as if they owned the place.

By mid-afternoon, when Mr Brant arrived, the front drive was raked out reasonably well. The tractor still stood on the same spot.

'Don't you worry about a little thing like that!' Mr Brant laughed. 'It's just the fuel that needs topping up. There's a spare can in the garage. I'll mow out the line before I go. Grass needed cutting anyway.'

He couldn't have been kinder. Had he shown them the water heater? Had he told them when the dustmen came? Did they know about the loose handle on the door of the bathroom?

After Mr Brant had finished the lawn, Simon's father gave him an envelope containing sixty pounds.

'Very reasonable too,' he said, 'for a week in a lovely place like this.'

'Well,' Mr Brant said, 'it is September, you know.'

'All the same!'

'Oh, there is just one other thing. I don't think I told you – the place is up for sale. There's a young couple who'd like to call round next week.'

Mr Langley nodded. As soon as he heard the words 'for sale', his eyes had lit up.

'They've seen the place once already and they're definitely interested. They would like just one last look though, before they make a definite offer. Next Thursday. Early afternoon. I hope that won't be a nuisance.'

'Heaven on earth!' Mr Langley muttered. 'This place is like heaven on earth – and only an hour's drive from Ipswich! *Heaven on earth*!'

'I hope you don't mind my asking,' he added loudly, 'but what's your selling price?'

'Well, I was hoping for thirty-two thousand. They've offered me thirty.'

'Well, of course I'll show them round.'

'No need to. Just let 'em take a look for themselves.' Suddenly the smile left Brant's face. 'And since you agree that you're getting a cheap holiday . . . there's no need to talk to them . . . no need to say a thing.'

'Thirty thousand pounds!' Mr Langley repeated. 'That's peanuts for a place like this.'

Brant left at four o'clock. Once he had gone, the family felt at home again. Dorothy Langley, as relaxed as her husband, had kicked off her shoes and now walked around the garden bare-footed. Though the afternoon grew cool, Mr Langley dozed on the lawn, his shirt rolled up to pillow the back of his head. Thirty thousand pounds. They could sell their Brayford house for forty!

'And what would you do for a job?' his wife laughed.

'Who needs work?' Barry Langley answered. 'I could always buy up an extra bit of land and have a bash at market-gardening.'

He could plant a rose garden just for his wife. From the oak tree he'd hang a swing for Emily. Make a change from his job at the cement works! The countryside would suit Simon, too. Life could be slow, deep and rich.

As Mr Langley daydreamed on his back, Simon watched the baby. She crawled round and round on the new-mown grass. He made sure she didn't eat worms.

Corner by corner, wall by wall, the room surprised Mrs Langley. She sat up in bed. There was Emily asleep in her cot: that was just the same. Yet, as she peered through the half-light, she needed a few seconds to find her bearings. The window seemed to be on the wrong side. A wardrobe, tall and dark, stood in place of her dressing-table. Also her back ached slightly: the bed was definitely harder than the one they had in Brayford.

Something else was different.

Mrs Langley glanced at her husband's socks, slung over the back of a chair. Really! Was that necessary? Couldn't he have pushed them into his shoes? At least he might have left them on the far side of the room.

Really!

It wasn't pleasant.

He would never have done that when they were first married. He seemed so careless now. She wanted to slip back beneath the blankets. But no ... she must open a window.

In fact the socks weren't as bad as she thought. Emily! That was it! She needed changing, poor little mite. She must be uncomfortable. Lying her on the empty half of the bed, Mrs Langley removed the nappy. Emily smiled. The smell of cleansing cream was everywhere – at least for the time being.

It was odd that Simon had got dressed so early. She found him in the kitchen.

'What are you doing?' she asked him.

'I'm just ... pulling out the fridge.'

'Why?'

'In case something dropped ... behind it.'

'You mean ...'

'Like old cabbage leaves or maybe a dead mouse.'

The fridge slid away from the wall. Simon peered round

the back. There was nothing but dust, an old key and an envelope.

'No luck, Mum. But surely *you* can smell it too.'

Mrs Langley nodded.

Then her husband walked in from the garden, wearing his pyjamas.

'Can *you* smell it, Dad?'

'Well? Can you, Barry?'

'Of course I can!' Mr Langley said. 'No two ways about it!'

'Maybe there's something wrong with the drains,' his wife suggested.

'I wouldn't be surprised. You never know with these country places. Some of them aren't even connected to the sewage system. There could be a septic tank somewhere. Nothing wrong with the front drains. I'm going to check the back garden.'

'Well, at least get dressed before you go out again.'

Mr Langley did not reply.

'Don't you want some breakfast first?'

'Oh dear, no! I'd much rather sort out . . . Oh heavens! It's getting worse every minute. Come on, Simon. You can give me a hand.'

The back garden, south-east of the house, was bathed in sunlight. But, for all its brightness, the air was far from pure.

'You see how the ground slopes away?' Simon's father explained. 'That means the drains must be laid down this way. If we search down by the pear tree, we might find a septic tank.'

'What does a septic tank look like, Dad?'

'It doesn't look like anything. It's buried underground.'

'Well, how will we know if it's there?'

'Look for a cover. A large, metal cover.'

Walking down to the lower end, they searched for metal amongst the weeds and overgrown grass.

'I think we're getting warmer, Dad!' Robert complained.

They continued their search with hands over noses.

Behind them, the lawn glistened more like a lake than land. Simon noticed their own footprints in the dew and, close to them, some starlings squabbling over breakfast. Pigeons – fat from unharvested raspberries – cooed amongst the soft-fruit bushes while, from hedges all about them, small birds sang descant.

It was a real paradise.

'By heck!' moaned Mr Langley. 'It's come on strong again!'

But an earthly paradise now, with a definite taint of hell.

Hard as they searched, they could find no septic tank. No heap of fresh compost. No dead animal. No explanation.

Mr Langley's slippers were soaked. They ate their bacon and eggs in the kitchen – but only after making sure every door and window was closed.

After breakfast they drove to Diss to buy some milk and a Sunday paper. They returned at about twelve o'clock. It was most odd.

They stood on the driveway and sniffed the air. The strongest smell was of mown grass. Simon walked past the copper beech. As he stood on the back lawn, he breathed in deeply. The air that he breathed was pure.

So the Langleys were even more astounded when the smell returned the next morning. Emily woke at seven o'clock. Mrs Langley changed her. They kept the doors and windows shut and, at eight-thirty, made for the car.

By the time they returned the odour had gone. They ate outside and dozed through the afternoon, sunbathing on the lawn.

Tuesday, Wednesday – the pattern was the same. They shrugged their shoulders and shook their heads. What could they do but accept the situation?

'No wonder this place is rented out cheap!' Mrs Langley kept saying. 'Half the normal price! I'm not surprised. It's not a holiday. Not in my opinion. It's more like half a holiday!'

There was no more talk of moving house. Maybe Mr Langley still daydreamed in the afternoons; but he never once mentioned selling up at Brayford, growing roses for his wife or the market-garden scheme.

The pattern of their days – shaped by the morning pestilence – did not change till the Thursday morning. At eight-thirty they went to the car. Simon said he wasn't coming.

'Are you ill or something?' his mother asked.

'No.'

'Well then, get in.'

'We'll all be ill if we don't clear out fast,' gasped Mr Langley from behind the steering wheel.

'You can stay if you want,' Simon's mother said, 'but are you sure you'll be all right by yourself?'

Simon was sure. He wanted to be alone. Alone except for the odour.

As soon as the car passed through the gate, he went down to the lower end of the back garden. For some reason he imagined a body in the hedge, but then pushed the idea from his mind. There were other things to worry about. Whether his parents had forgotten about the house sale or whether they were just pretending to forget, he could not be certain. But *he* remembered all right. He remembered overhearing his dad and Brant. Maybe he *was* slow, but that didn't mean he was stupid. In particular, he recalled the moment Brant scowled and said, 'You're getting a cheap holiday... no need to talk to them . . . no need to say a thing.'

And though he had not yet met the couple, he already felt sorry for them.

There was not much point in searching the garden again. For a moment he was tempted to go back indoors. He could lie down on his bed. He could think a bit. If he didn't come up with any bright ideas, he could have a little snooze before his family returned.

Then, quite suddenly – as if by mistake – Simon reached a decision. For the first time – trips into Diss didn't count – he was going to leave the garden. Turning back through the vegetable patch, he pushed his way through nettles. He clambered up the steep slope towards the little copse. His parents had forgotten the most important thing of all: they were not in a village, but in countryside! A minute later he was pushing his way through brambles and hazel. He was still panting heavily when he at last stood on the brink of an outside world. To his right he caught sight of a meandering river, lined with trees. He thought they were probably willows. In the sunlight their leafage seemed white, green and silvery, all at the same time. Cattle grazed. It was like a painting. Everything distanced and still.

What broke the spell was a squeal.

Yes! A squeal! Then another! Much closer than he expected. From higher ground, to the left, he thought he heard men's voices. The sound of metal clank-clanking and then more squeals. High squeals. Low grunts too, when he listened more carefully. There was no doubt now. No more than fifty yards away, a vast grey building of sheet metal. That was it then! That was it!

He was staring straight at a pig farm.

They ate lunch outdoors as usual. Nobody spoke very much.

'A piggery! A piggery!' Mr Langley muttered as he finished his ham salad.

'You did say Thursday, didn't you, Barry?'

'Sorry?'

'The young couple. Remember? Today! This afternoon!'

'Of course I remembered, Dorothy!'

Simon glanced at his father.

'You will tell them, won't you, Dad!'

'Oh, I'll tell them all right – as soon as they arrive.'

Mrs Langley stood up. She had finished eating. She said she was going to tidy up a bit. Simon was surprised. He couldn't see the point.

'Why bother to tidy up?' said her husband, as if he could read Simon's thoughts. 'We're not going to let them buy the place!'

But Mrs Langley had made up her mind. She wasn't going to have people thinking they lived like animals, even if they were on holiday.

At half-past three a smart blue car drew up at the side of the house. Brian Culvert stood at the end of the cottage, surveying the garden at the front and back. His wife, Celia, poked her tongue behind her top lip, pushed it outward and removed a speck of stray lipstick with her hanky. As they walked round to the front, her foot caught in a nasty rut. It was one of the furrows made by Mr Langley when he had mowed the gravel. 'Steady, dear!' Brian Culvert said, as she jolted against him. Both of them wore tinted glasses with thin, rectangular frames. The lenses were dark as they stood in the afternoon sun.

'Hello. It's so good of you to let us have a look round. Mr Brant said you knew ...'

'Yes. That's right,' Mr Langley said. 'It's just that ... Well, to be quite honest, we thought we ought to explain ...'

'Now, don't you worry about us. Celia and I have really fallen for the place. We just wanted a last look before it's all signed and sealed.'

'Yes, but it might be in your interest ...'

'No, no, Mr Langley. The last thing we want to do is interrupt your holiday.'

And before they could stop them, the couple were off round the gardens. The Langleys stared at each other helplessly and walked into the kitchen.

'In a minute,' said Mr Langley, 'they'll want to see inside. That'll be the moment to tell them.'

If only the couple had come in the morning! Or if only the smell would return! You could photograph places and record sounds. But how, Simon wondered, could you capture a smell? He knew that his mind was rambling.

'Absolutely heavenly!'

'What a gorgeous setting!'

The young couple had walked into the kitchen.

'As a point of interest,' Mr Langley began, 'did you ... I wonder if ... as a point of interest ...'

Suddenly Simon felt sorry for his father. The words

would sound so awful. He didn't envy him.

'Yes?' Brian Culvert prompted.

'Well ... Oh look! Your glasses have gone clear. I do find that interesting!'

'Barry! That's personal!' Mrs Langley objected.

'Not at all!' said Mr Culvert. 'They are rather interesting aren't they! They're made by a firm called Reactolite. Very clever really. The tint darkens up in sunlight and then clears in the shade. Cost the earth. But Celia and I are quite satisfied. Our eyes are very sensitive, you see.'

Simon wondered how sensitive their noses were. Pig muck! They were going to wake up to it! Reactolite lenses wouldn't help much there. What on earth were his parents playing at?

Too late now. The next moment, the young couple were walking upstairs. Mr and Mrs Langley sat down at the table.

'I've got it! said his mother. 'We'll ask them to tea. They can stay for tea! We'll have tea on the lawn. Yes! That'll be lovely!'

'Good idea, Dorothy. It would be kinder. I can sort of break it to them gently.'

Twenty minutes later they all sat at the garden table. Simon's mother poured the tea. 'That's better!' she kept saying. 'This was such a good idea. That's better. Now do help yourself to biscuits.' In an odd sort of way, she seemed to be acting – almost as if she owned the place. The lady of the manor.

'It's not definite!' Simon's father suddenly blurted out.

'I beg your pardon?'

'The house. You know. You did say you hadn't actually signed any papers!'

'No,' said Brian Culvert. 'But I really can't see anything to make us change our minds. It's bliss! Sheer bliss!'

'Well . . . How about another slice of cake?'

Through the upstairs window they heard Emily crying. Mr Langley was on his feet in seconds. Mrs Langley said, 'Excuse me – the teapot needs a little more hot water.' Simon Langley wanted to go, but forced himself to stay seated.

'And how are you enjoying your holiday?'

'Up and down!' the boy muttered. He was starting to sweat. He'd already eaten six biscuits and three almond slices.

'Do you like the cottage?' Mr Culvert asked.

'Yes . . .'

'That's good.'

'. . . and no!'

'I'm sorry?'

'I like it . . . in the afternoons.'

'What a strange thing to say!' Mrs Culvert exclaimed. 'You mean you don't like it in the evening.

'Yes. I mean, no! I like it in the evenings and the afternoons. But I don't . . . I don't like it in the mornings.'

The Culverts glanced at each other through their Reactolite lenses which were now very dark in the sunshine.

'And why don't you like it . . . in the mornings?'

Simon reached for the last almond slice. Then, with enormous effort, he put it back on the plate.

'It pongs,' he said.

They hadn't understood.

'Pongs! Pongs! You know! . . . *Pongs!*'

Mrs Culvert laughed nervously.

'All babies smell a little, dear!'

'Not the baby. The piggery! It pongs!'

'Pongs?'

'Yes!'

'Piggery?'

'Yes! The piggery! It pongs!'

41

Simon's throat ached. He grabbed the almond slice. But now he had lost all appetite.

'I'll fetch my dad. He'll tell you.'

But there was no need to fetch him. Mr Langley stood behind his son.

'Thank you, Simon,' he said. His nerve had returned. 'Mr and Mrs Culvert, please listen carefully. I think the time has come . . .'

Passing his mother and Emily on the stairs, Simon went up to lie on his bed. He gave way to a wave of exhaustion. When he awoke, the Culverts had gone.

Brant rang the same evening. The house sale was off.

'Please vacate the premises by twelve o'clock this Saturday,' he added.

Dad said he sounded like a different man.

As it happened, the Langleys were ready to leave well before nine.

'Come on, Simon. Don't just stand there dawdling!' his mother said. Then his father passed by with the carrycot. The boy suddenly realized that the moment would never be lost. A crumbling wall, the trellised roses, pig smells in the morning sun.

'Simon! Simon! You're daydreaming again!'

He thought of their house on Brayford Main Street.

It was good to be going back home.

The following year was a bad one for pork. The bottom fell out of the market. Three months later the farmer sold up.

The next owner tried market-gardening.

Niners are Nothing

Sally Warder could not help herself.

She knew it was not the sort of thing girls did. Her young brother, Philip, did it, of course. But now he had gone on ahead, leaving her with her friend, Rachel. Beneath the conker tree, Rachel was impatient as well.

'Come on, Sally! I've got to take registers round before school starts. Come on! I can't wait all day.'

Sally did not answer. There was plenty of time for registers. Anyhow, she would only be a moment.

Funny, she thought, how you always forget with conkers. Not the conkers themselves, but the green spiky casing. Every autumn, the smell of their moist, white lining came as a surprise.

'Sally! Right! That's it – I told you I'm not waiting.'

There! Just ahead, to the right! That was a beauty, that one!

Rachel had gone on. Sally looked across the Lower Green and saw her friend overtake Philip. That wasn't difficult since the seven-year-old had flung his PE bag down and was now sitting on it. Sally decided he could wait a minute. She would savour a few more moments alone.

She bent down, careful that neither her knees nor her skirt touched the damp grass. Then – almost with a feeling of guilt – she picked up another conker. Her mouth opened slightly as she turned it in her fingers. It was like polished leather, except that it was even harder and smoother. Very flat and almost white, the top was. As she looked at it from above, the ochre sides bulged out – perfect, generous and round. She turned the conker one more time – Philip was on his feet again – and almost wished it could have stayed in its shell. Maybe sunlight did it. Maybe old age. Either way they all lost their shine and darkened up in the end. Unzipping her jacket pocket, she popped the conker in. She didn't collect that many conkers, but she was going to keep this one.

Behind her she heard leaves rustle. It was Brenton Sheen.

'What are you doing here?' he asked.

Brenton wasn't a bad sort. But lately he'd fallen in with the school bully, Dean Fulcher.

'Yeah. What are you up to?' Dean snapped, as if Sally were trespassing.

She did not answer.

'Look, Dean! Look!' Brenton shouted.

'What's the matter?'

'Goddawoppa! Goddawoppa!'

'Bigguns crack easier,' said the bully, shrugging.

'We'll see about that later!'

One of the boys then found a dead branch. They kicked it, jumped on it, stood on it and pulled it till finally it cracked. They spent the next few minutes hurling it upward, stopping only when Rebecca Starling walked by with her mother. They started again as soon as the mother and daughter had gone.

'You want to be careful!' a third boy shouted. It was

another top Junior – Melvyn Maddock. 'My cousin was chucking sticks once and one came down on the main road right on top of a bus and the driver stopped but he couldn't get off the bus and leave all the passengers, so my cousin just ran off.'

Dean Fulcher looked at him.

'That's nothing. My elder brother, Tim, once did worse than that. He used to chuck stones and once one went over our neighbour's fence and he'd just bought this little statue of a woman with no clothes on for his garden pond and it hit her on the kneecap and chipped it and my dad had to buy another one and he didn't half give my brother what for!'

'What?' asked Melvyn. 'You mean he went to a shop and said, "Excuse me. Can I please have a new kneecap for a nude lady?"?'

They laughed. Then Brenton said. 'That's nothing, 'cos two years ago, when we lived in Ipswich, my dad . . .'

The three of them walked off, chatting and laughing. As soon as he saw them, Philip ran back towards Sally, dragging his PE bag through the wet grass. She looked at the ground beneath the tree for one last time. There was the boys' stick and, close to it, another green sphere. Conkers didn't grow on trees: they grew in green, spiky cases on trees. Picking it up, she was startled by the bitter-sweet smell again. It was already split. A boy had taken the conker from it. That would be split too, before long.

Philip was tugging at her coat.

'That's nothing. That's empty,' he said.

Funny with boys, Sally thought. With boys everything was nothing. That's nothing – I did this! That's nothing – I did that! Football, conkers, swimming, fishing – somebody had to be top dog. Somebody had to win.

She closed her hand around the broken casing and

laughed as she felt the points against her palm – no fiercer than the nip of a puppy or a kitten. Dropping it, she thought of the perfect conker in her pocket. She checked her watch and knew they would be late again.

'One more time,' Mrs Winters said, 'and you'll be taking a letter home! As it is, you can stand in the deputy's office at playtime.'

'Well, at least . . .' Sally thought, at the beginning of playtime. 'Well, at least . . .'

She always did that. Whenever she got punished, at home or at school, she always did her best to think up a little advantage. In winter, at least she'd be in the warm. In summer, at least she'd cool down. Since September, it had been easy. Any time she was kept in, at least her brother couldn't plague her. Everybody laughed when she said he was a pest. But Sally wasn't joking. In September he'd moved up to a Junior class. So things were even worse now, because he shared the same playground.

'Why didn't you tell the teacher?'

'I did and she told me to tell you.'

'Well, if the boys push you over, don't play with them.'

'But it was my football!'

Then there was the time he lost his shoe. She could still remember him hopping across the playground in tears.

'Well, why don't you just go and put on your plimsolls?'

'Boowoowoo . . . 'cos I left them at home.'

Well, at least today, as she stood in the safety of Mrs Rudge's office . . .

'Sally! Sally!'

Philip staggered into the room.

'I can't talk to you now, Philip. I'm kept in. I can't talk to anyone.'

'But . . . But Dean Fulcher took my conker. He stole it!

46

That was a niner!'

'Why didn't you tell the teacher?'

'Did.'

'And?'

'She asked Dean and Dean swore he never.'

'Well, stop crying, for heaven's sake!'

'Can't!'

'Why not?'

'I can't . . . 'cos my throat is hurting.'

'Well, it might stop hurting if you just stop crying.'

'It won't. I know it won't!'

A tear hit the floor between the two children. Then another. They shone like ten-pence pieces on the grey tiling.

Mrs Rudge appeared and said Sally could go out for the last five minutes. She put an arm around Philip's shoulder.

'Been in the wars again, have you?'

She asked Sally to keep an eye on him.

It was probably the only time in the year when no football was played on the playground. Girls showed a grudging interest in conkers, watching it now and again – but only from a distance. Elastics and skipping kept some of them busy. The younger girls tooted recorders.

But odd things happened to the boys. Tall strikers destined for the first division; goalkeepers; stone-wall defenders – suddenly it was all one. They roamed the playground in search of easy prey for their fivers and six-ers. First year or fourth year, it didn't matter any more. Melvyn Maddock – the strongest boy in the school, Bren-ton Sheen – the fastest, Dean Fulcher – the most vicious, all stood face to face with timid young midgets. Many con-tests lasted only seconds. Shells split and the tarmac was sprayed with white fragments. Groups of children broke and re-formed. A bad shot meant laces or string tangled up and Melvyn shouting 'Stringses!' like an Infant. Sometimes a conker would slip over a knot. You were allowed to crush those; but even Dean would squeal 'Stampses!' before he put the boot in.

Fourth-year girls, calm in their pleated skirts, looked down on it all with smiles and shakes of the head. The boys were at it again. Perhaps they couldn't help it. Anyway, in five minutes they'd be back in class, working at area, volume and fractions. Back to their own age again.

Now Philip also stood and watched. He reached up and pulled on Sally's arm.

'Blow your nose,' she said.

He sniffed.

'I didn't say sniff it. I said blow it!'

Then Dean Fulcher swaggered past.

'I got a niner!' he taunted. Sally knew he did it on purpose.

Philip said he hadn't got a Kleenex.

'We are the champions!' Dean Fulcher sang.

When Sally walked up to him, he giggled in her face.

'My brother wants his niner back.'

Dean looked up in the air, then slowly raised his hand.

Between them, the conker swung on its string. Several other boys came round. Dean giggled as Sally stepped closer.

'Why don't you run along, Sally? Play a game of elastics or something.'

Sally stretched her hand out and waited. The conker swung from side to side, just six inches above it.

'Mummy asked for her elastic back, did she?' Dean grinned and reddened as he said it. 'You stole Mummy's elastic, didn't you, and now her knickers keep falling down!'

Still the conker and string swung like a pendulum. Side to side. Side to side.

Sally turned away, suddenly defeated. Philip, a few yards from her, stared at his big sister as if she had failed him again. And it was true – something about Dean really frightened her. A minute part of him, knotted up, that would never grow. That was why larger, stronger boys always backed off. They would no more choose to fight Dean Fulcher than a rabbit would a ferret.

She wanted to walk off, but made herself face him again. For the first time she saw how small Dean was. It had nothing to do with inches.

One eye half-closed, he cocked his head to the side. On the end of its string, the conker still swung – no faster, no slower.

Sally was surprised by a movement to her right. Melvyn Maddock – the nearest Dean had to a friend – spoke quietly:

'Go on, Dean. Give it back.'

Simon Langley then sauntered up, followed by Brenton Sheen. Some girls as well – Sandra Harris, the Wright twins and Sally's friend, Rachel Conners.

'Come on, Dean!' It was Brenton this time. 'That's Philip's conker. You know it is! We saw you take it from him.'

Dean did not answer. He just glowered at Sally. She stared back, knowing there was no right or wrong now – just her against him.

All over the playground, conker games were abandoned. Even the girls stopped chatting and skipping. By the time Mrs Winters blew the whistle, it was too late: a crowd of children stood around Sally and Dean. Then Mrs Winters called for Class 4L to go in. Nobody moved. Nobody spoke. It had gone too far for anybody to turn their backs on the scene. Too many memories of shins Dean had kicked, arms he had twisted or bitten. Too many thumped backs. Too many pictures splattered with paint, lunch boxes pilfered, shoes hidden. Too many Infant brothers and sisters tripped up in the dining room.

Mrs Winters walked up closer to the circle.

'4L. Go on in now, please ... What on earth is going on?'

The slap that Sally delivered caught Dean on the right cheek. His jaw dropped open.

The niner hit the ground, its thin trail of string flipping behind it as it bounced a few feet across the tarmac. Not a sound after that. Not even when it had settled.

Nobody knew if the boy or the girl moved first – only that the circle broke and Sally, hair flying back, darted out. Dean was through the gap she made before it could close again. Mrs Winters lunged, but missed him.

Sally ran right round the edge of the playground, the boy no more than six feet behind her. Already she imagined the tug on the back of her coat, then Dean's grip on her arm as he swung her round and round.

Passing the school gate for the second time, she glanced behind her. Dean was no longer there. She then understood that his eyes were still on her. He stood opposite Sally, on the far side of the crowd. Impossible to tell at what moment he'd move. Children shifted uneasily, afraid that he would suddenly try to cut a passage through them. Then he did move – very slowly, and in the same direction as before. He broke into a run. Mrs Winters shouted, but it made no difference. Both children were sprinting round again.

'I'll get you ... you little ... I'll get you!' he spluttered. Sally passed the gate a third and fourth time. She gasped for breath. Burning! Her lungs seemed to be burning! She felt a heavy sickness in her stomach, as if she'd already been hit.

'I'll get you!' Another stream of insults spilt out of the bully. And then, quite unexpectedly, Sally remembered the conker. Not Philip's conker. Her own. She knew it was there, zipped up in her pocket. No need to look. No need to touch it. It was still there. It had been there all the time, round and perfect.

'You just wait! I'll give you such a ...'

For the first time, she realized that she could win. Dean's own anger would be his worst enemy. He should have been saving his breath for running. Suddenly her feet seemed to bounce off the ground. She could almost have laughed. She passed the gate again. A fifth lap. A sixth. Effortless. Round and perfect. Perfect and round.

51

Even before she stopped, she knew Dean had given up. She looked for him, but all she saw was the backs of 120 children. She realized that they were all staring out of the school grounds. Dean Fulcher had not stopped running – he had simply carried on in a straight line. By now he had passed through the school gate. They watched him grow smaller and smaller as he ran towards home.

Sally stood still. She breathed quite freely. Some of the younger children were clapping. One by one they all filed in, till at last there was no one left on the tarmac. Just Sally, her brother and the teacher.

'I'm sorry, Miss.'

'It wasn't your fault, Sally,' Mrs Winters said quietly. Sally knew she was right. She found the niner, picked it up and handed it to her brother.

'That's yours, Philip.'

'I'll keep it,' the boy said, his eyes full of admiration. 'I won't use that one for conker fights.'

Mrs Winters smiled and went in to tell the headteacher about the child who'd run home.

'Too good to smash up, that one is!' Philip added as they followed her in.

'But I thought it was a niner and that you'd use it again. I thought that was the whole idea – it was going to be a champion.'

Philip reached into his pocket and pulled at a length of string.

'Not really. That's only a niner. Look at this one, Sally! This one's a twelver already! That one there is only a niner. Niners are nothing!'

Sally didn't mind.

She put a hand in her pocket. She would not show her conker to anyone.

Dead Rockets Don't Fly

'Got another!' Philip shouted.

The two girls, Sally and Rachel, did not seem very interested. There might still be a further half hour of sunlight, but the east wind was bitterly cold.

'What on earth does he want with dead rockets, anyway?' Sally wondered.

'I don't know. He's *your* brother,' Rachel replied.

The boy ran up to them.

'And another! Look!'

He pushed the rocket so close to Sally's face that the empty tube almost touched her nose.

'Come on, Philip! We're frozen stiff. Two more minutes and we're going home.'

The boy ran round to the other side of the bonfire, rocket sticks jutting out of both his pockets. It was November 6th. Twenty-three hours had passed since it was lit, yet the charred remains still smouldered.

'Funny thing!' Sally said. 'It's funny how dead rockets don't bust up. I mean they must come down forty or fifty feet and yet most of them end up perfect. Empty, but perfect.'

Rachel, older and slightly taller than Sally, had moved into Brayford only a few weeks ago. Already she was Sally's closest friend. She bent down to pick up a dead rocket herself.

'Did he collect them last year?' she asked.

'No.'

'Well, he's making up for it now. Just look at him!'

Both of them laughed as Philip reappeared. Despite the cold, he had unzipped his coat and stuck four or five more sticks inside the belt of his trousers. He looked like a human pincushion.

'Mustn't fall down or the sticks'll stab my tummy,' he declared earnestly.

Sally said not to be so silly and to zip up his coat. But before they could stop him, he had run off again.

'Come on, you twit! Come on! You've got enough!'

It made no difference. Staring at the smouldering bonfire, the sister became more serious. A frown wrinkled her forehead.

'Sally! What are you looking so worried about? We'll be leaving in a minute.'

'Dog basket,' the blonde girl muttered.

'What did you say?'

'The dog basket.'

'Well, if anyone chucked a dog basket on that bonfire, there wouldn't be much of it left this evening! Wicker would burn in seconds, it would.'

'Not last night Rachel, but a whole year ago. I'll never forget last year's Guy Fawkes. Oscar died just a few days before.'

'Who was Oscar? An uncle?'

'No, no. Oscar – our dog.'

Sally turned towards her friend. Quiet sort of person, Rachel was. She never talked very much, yet she felt so close to her.

'Go on, Sally,' she said. 'Go on, Sally. I'm listening.'

Well, he was fantastic. A crossbred. Two dogs for the price of one, Dad used to say. He claimed that Oscar was a very rare animal: nobody else in England, much less in Brayford, had a wire-haired fox-poodle!

'What did he die of!'

'Liver.'

'What's wrong with liver?'

No, no – his liver. It had stopped working properly. Dad took him down to the vet on the Friday evening and I went with them. When we got back to the car twenty minutes later – without Oscar – we could hardly believe it had happened. It was dark by then, and drizzling. "With any luck," Dad mumbled, "Philip will be fast asleep by now. Maybe Mum can tell him in the morning."

At breakfast, on the Saturday, Philip never noticed that the dog wasn't around. He was still only six, you see. Afterwards he asked if he could go with Dad when he took Oscar out for his walk. Mum said very quietly – but no two ways about it – "They put Oscar to sleep last night."

"Well, let's wake him up!" Philip said.

Dad left half his breakfast and went out to the garden.

When Mum tried again, Philip just shrugged his shoulders and pouted up his mouth. He didn't cry. Mum said to hurry up and we could all drive up to Ipswich to buy some extra fireworks. I didn't think Philip had heard her properly. But suddenly he sat down in the middle of the kitchen floor and kicked his heels against the tiles.

That was the nearest we got to fireworks that Saturday!

Do you think I didn't want to cry myself? Of course I did. But I was already a Third Year Junior. Third Year Juniors don't cry, do they! That's what I told myself, anyway.

All through Saturday lunch, Philip stared at Dad as if he'd been the cause of death. Later on, we went to the living room and watched the racing on telly. Mum and Dad hate the racing. So do Philip and I. We watched the whole lot that afternoon.

Sunday was just the same, except we watched a black-and-white film instead.

None of us ever thought he would keep it up so long. The silence, I mean. Worst of all, that silence seemed to take hold of us all in the end.

As we ate our evening meal, the only noise was the tea being poured and the clink of knives and forks on the plates. Philip gulped his food and then went up to his bedroom for about the twentieth time.

I heard Mum whisper something to Dad.

"What?"

"The basket, Peter. We'll have to get rid of the basket."

There it was, in the corner of the kitchen, Oscar's old torn blanket still ruffled up inside it.

"You're quite right," says Dad. "I'll take it out and leave it by the bins."

Mum told him he wasn't thinking straight. The dustmen wouldn't be calling till Wednesday. Even then, they might not take it away.

"Well, in that case," he says, "I'll take it over to the Lower Green and put it on the bonfire."

He told us not to worry. He'd hide it really well – under an old door or something. I reckon that's what he did. Anyway, the basket disappeared that evening.

The kitchen looked horribly big without it.

On the Monday, Philip said he felt sick. Mum said he could stay at home. Dad would never have agreed to that but, of course, he'd already left for work.

When I got back from school, the kitchen still looked empty. Then Dad came in and you could see straight away that his temper was just terrible. Philip wouldn't eat his tea and Mum started to explain how he'd missed school. That was all Dad needed. You should have heard him slam his hand on the table! I reckon the cups jumped out of the saucers.

Wham!

"What on earth's got into you all?" he shouted. "Philip says he's too ill to go to school and you actually believe him! For heaven's sake, the whole thing's ridiculous. It's only an animal that died! An animal – not a person! An animal that was old and ill! An animal! Just an animal!"

Philip was terrified. None of us even tried to stop him when he ran for his bedroom. Mum and I just sat at the table. Dad paced to the living room and back. This time we could hear Philip upstairs. There was no doubt about it – he was crying.

"Best thing," Mum said. "That's the best thing that could happen."

I didn't cry. I think I told you that. But I didn't sleep either. It must have been about two o'clock in the morning – and I just lay there thinking. Don't ask me why, but I suddenly remembered something. Stupid, really. But I suddenly remembered all the tins of dog food stacked up in the kitchen cupboard. As long as they were there, I knew that nothing would change. Tuesday would be just the same as Monday, Sunday and Saturday. I couldn't bear it. I had to put on my dressing-gown. I had to go down to look in the cupboard . . .

Even before I reached the hallway, I knew there was a light on in the kitchen. But I was still startled when I saw Dad, sitting at the table alone.

Beyond him – on the table itself – all the tins of dog food stood in a pyramid. He placed the last tin on the very top. For at least a minute, neither of us moved. Then Dad scratched his head – I remember that – just on the bald patch at the back. I wondered what made him play with those tins. Like a child, he was. Playing with bricks. Then I saw that his shoulders were shaking. Maybe if I had just walked up closer . . . Maybe if I had raised a hand and laid it on his shoulder . . .

I just left. I never made a sound.

Passing Philip's door, on the way back to my bedroom, I wanted to wake him up. I wanted to tell him what I'd seen. I wanted to tell him that, even if Dad had shouted, that didn't mean . . . But what was the use? How could a boy of six really understand?

The next morning all the tins had gone – no doubt into the dustbin. Mum and Dad seemed very calm. Then Philip sat on Dad's knee and the two of them were smiling. "We know! We both know!" their smiles seemed to say. "But from now on we won't even mention him!"

"Well, I know too!" I wanted to shout. "Do you think I don't feel the same?"

Dad bounced Philip up and down. I don't know why, but I wanted to be bounced, too. Then I realized Dad had to get to work. Anyway, I was far too old – too old for that sort of thing. It seemed best to leave it at that. Sometimes it's best to let things slide – just let things slide, if you can.'

Suddenly Philip rushed up to them. He was panting and laughing and trying to talk, all at the same time.

'I got loads and loads and loads.'

'Good, 'cos it's time to go home.'

'Just two more minutes! Go on, Sally! You said two minutes!'

'That was five minutes ago. Come on!'

'Oh, bluver!'

Rachel giggled at the boy's swear-word – a mixture of bother, bloody and oh brother.

'Bluver! Bluver! Bluver and blast!' Philip shouted. He threw several dead rockets up into the air, stamped a foot and started crying.

'You are not going to get your way,' Sally stated quietly. 'And it's no good throwing those things about. Dead rockets don't fly anyway.'

'And bluver you too!' Philip cursed.

He then swore that he would not walk a step further.

'Well, we're not going to carry you!' said Sally. 'You'll just have to wait here all night. We'll collect you tomorrow morning. No doubt you'll be frozen stiff by then. But we can always thaw you out in time for school on Monday.'

Two more rockets were flung upward. They spun pathetically and landed with a thud.

'Come on, Rachel,' Sally whispered. 'Just keep walking. We'll wait for him by the Ipswich Road. You'll see – he won't be long.'

Two minutes later they reached the road bridge that marked the north-east corner of the Lower Green.

'And did you?' Rachel asked.

'Did I *what*?'

'Did you let it slide and just forget about Oscar?'

Some people had a talent for talk: Rachel had a talent for listening.

'No. Not really. It wasn't as simple as that. Where did I get to? Oh yes – the next thing was Guy Fawkes Night. It was the same plan as usual. Dad won't have fireworks in the garden. Says they're far too expensive – you get nothing for five pounds. That's why we go down to the Lower Green. Everyone shares their fireworks here, so you get a real display. We've done it like that for years.

"Fabulous bonfire!" Dad promised, and we all knew it was true. I'm not joking. If you thought last night's bonfire was big, you should have seen it last year! Last year's had a whole tree in it – an elm that had died of disease. They started it in September and, by the time they had finished, it was almost the height of a building. Honestly! They had to use a ladder when it came to putting on the Guy.

But every time I saw it or even thought of it, I couldn't help remembering old Oscar's basket. I didn't know exactly how or when Dad did it, but the basket was in there somewhere.

"Don't worry about the rolls," Mum said on November 5th. "I'll get them this morning. All you have to do is call

60

in at Maddock's and pick up the sausages on the way back from work tonight."

Dad said, fine. He'd also get a large bag of charcoal. He said he didn't care how cold it was, he was going to barbecue the sausages out in the garden.

At first I couldn't understand what all the fuss was about. Then I realized. A party! A party, would you believe it, back at our house afterwards! So that's what they were planning. Hot dogs! Drinks! Dozens of people!

"We've got to cancel it!" I said. "Surely, if we explained about Oscar ... surely they'd have to understand."

Dad said seven or eight families were coming. We'd invited them weeks ago. We couldn't uninvite them.

All day at school, I was thinking about the dog. Philip seemed to have forgotten that Oscar ever existed.

On the way back home, he kept spinning round and round. I told him to walk straight.

"I can't, I can't," he whined.

"Why not?"

"'Cos I'm a Catherine Wheel."

Then he started jumping up and down and going whoosh like a madman. That's 'cos he was a Roman Candle. I could have clouted him.

Dad was back home by five, setting out glasses and paper plates and pricking his blessed sausages. You'd have thought Christmas had come six weeks too early. The bouncier they all got, the glummer I was feeling.

When everything was laid out for the party, we went off to the Lower Green. The fireworks were fantastic, it's true. As for the bonfire, they lit it just after we arrived. Within five minutes the flames must have been thirty feet high. (Afterwards some people even said that the glow could be seen from Brindlesham Hill – nearly five miles away.) Nobody stood very close. You couldn't. It was like

61

a furnace. As for me, I left the crowd, crossed the river by the footbridge and walked up to the Top Green. I remember that my feet were soaking wet because of the long grass. But the whole hillside seemed to be red and, when I turned round, my face was tingling: believe it or not, I was sweating. It was weird, Rachel. Really weird. The bonfire below seemed to dwarf everyone. To my mind, the grown-ups looked like children: the children looked more like pygmies.

"Oooh!" they all cooed when a rocket went up. "Aaah!" when it burst into a spray of coloured stars. "Oooh! Look at that! . . . Aaah! Did you see it? Oooh! Oooh! Aaah! . . ."

I felt like crying.

But I didn't. I went back to the crowd to find my family. Mum and Dad said we'd have to leave earlier than the others, to get the barbecue going. As we walked back, Philip whizzed and whirled all through the estate. I wanted to smack him as badly as before, but I knew it was wrong to blame him.

The first guests to arrive were the Sheens.

"Where's Oscar, then?" Mrs Sheen asked. "Nice and safe inside, I hope. I always feel so sorry for the animals."

I couldn't blame her, either. How was she to know, till Mum took her aside and explained?

Then there was Mr and Mrs Trinder, who'd come along with the Langleys.

"Nice joint of lamb we had yesterday," old Trinder said. "We thought to bring the bone along for Oscar."

It was wrapped in newspaper. Dad said, "Thank you, but . . ." He took the wrapped-up bone to the kitchen and dropped it into the bin.

I suppose my parents kept the party alive, though I didn't thank them for it. They smiled and chatted as the others came in. The Wright twins were there, the Dentons *and the Starlings, Paula and Melvyn Maddock and the Thomkins.*

*   Even when the guests left, Mum and Dad were still laughing. Dad especially. A silly, high laugh that didn't belong to him. Then Philip started to cry because there were no more sparklers and also because he'd eaten too many hot dogs and had a pain. Mum put him to bed and it was peaceful again.*

*   Now that it was quiet, I wanted to shout. I don't know why, Rachel, but I wanted to open my mouth and shout my head off . . . Instead, I went back to the garden.*

*   "You all right, Sally?" Dad asked gently.*

*   I couldn't answer. I just stared at the embers of charcoal. They were grey now, but still very warm.*

*   He poked them once or twice.*

*   "It'll be all right," he said.*

*   So I sat down on his knee and really hugged him.'*

Rachel, having listened, put a hand on Sally's shoulder.

'But all that was a year ago. You don't still think about Oscar, do you?'

'No. Not really. Only now and again.'

'So it was all right – like your dad said.'

'Of course it was. Most things are all right, with time.'

'Talking of time, don't you think we'd better go back for your brother?'

'Oh, him!' Sally giggled. 'I suppose you're right.'

Philip was messing about by the bonfire, two hundred feet away from them.

'What on earth's he up to now?' Rachel said.

'Heaven knows. He lives in a world of his own.'

The girls walked smartly towards the small boy. The story of a year ago echoed in their minds: the remains of last night's burning lay just before them. Nothing but ash and old nails now – charcoaled wood, an old kettle, the hub and spokes of a pram.

At the edge of the circle, a lost woollen glove.

Sally bent down and picked up a dead rocket.

'Don't bother telling Philip,' she said. 'He won't remember, and even if he did . . .'

Rachel noticed that Philip was busy. He too held a stick.

'Don't worry. I'll fetch him,' she said. Even before she reached the boy, she knew he'd been poking about in the ashes. Yet she was still surprised to see a shape, traced on to the ground.

It was a dog. A peculiar dog. The body was round and resembled a poodle. Yet it had a fox-terrier look as well – especially in the squareness of the head.

When he had finished it, Philip stood up straight, turned towards Rachel and smiled.

'Wire-haired fox-poodle,' he told her.

Rachel wanted to tell Sally – but in fact she said nothing.

The Other Christmas Man

Mrs Rudge bent down close to the girl. She wanted to make herself heard and yet to speak gently.

'Tummyache?' she asked. 'Don't you feel very well?'

She had been keeping an eye on Rebecca Starling for the last half hour. All through the party games, the little red-head had sat on a bench at the side of the school hall. It wasn't like her. It wasn't like Rebecca Starling at all. Normally she could not keep quiet or still. The sort of girl who would call out excitedly, even in the middle of Story. Yet all through the Infants' Christmas party she had sat on the bench as if musical chairs meant nothing to her. She had not even wanted to pass the parcel.

'You don't have to eat any more if your tummy feels funny,' Mrs Rudge explained. It wasn't worth ringing Rebecca's mother. Not now. In fifteen minutes the tea would be over. Father Christmas would be brought in, the children collected by their parents, and the hall cleared.

Next to Rebecca sat Jenny Wright, demolishing a pile of peanut-butter sandwiches. Just beyond Jenny sat Jodie Wright – her twin. She was squashing up jelly with the back of a spoon and mixing it into her ice-cream.

'Philip Warder fibs,' Jenny declared, when the teacher had moved away.

'He do! He do!' Jodie agreed. 'And even if his dog did die when they put him to sleep, that don't mean your tortoise have to die too.'

'That don't, Rebecca,' Jodie added. 'Tortoises are meant

to go to sleep. Loads of animals go to sleep in the winter. That's called hivermating.'

Neither of them could convince Rebecca. The truth was, they were not quite convinced themselves. Maybe Thomas the Second *was* dead. Maybe he would *never* wake up. It came to the same thing.

'You don't say *hivermate*, Jodie,' Jenny corrected her twin. 'You say *hibervate* – like squirrels eat nuts and hibervate.'

Rebecca didn't care very much. Hivermate or hibervate – what did it matter? How could anything matter, while Thomas slept on and on?

Once again she tried to explain her worries to the two Wright girls.

'When Philip's dog died last year, his mum said he'd been put to sleep. But when Philip told her it was time to wake him up, she just said he was dead. So when my dad went and put Thomas in a cardboard box in the shed, I got all worried and I asked Dad what on earth did he think he was doing, and he said Thomas was going to sleep for a long, long time – and that sounds like for ever to me!'

'Hibervation,' Jenny insisted.

'That's all,' Jodie added. 'Nothing but hivermation.' And as if that settled the matter for good, she turned her attention back to the jelly and ice-cream.

Jenny was having second thoughts.

'But you got to admit that mums do fib. They do fib sometimes. Don't you remember our mum once said we were going to the doctor's for tea? But when we got there Doctor Warren went and stuck a needle in our arms. I don't call that tea.'

'Yip, they do fib,' Jodie confirmed. 'Mummies fib. So do daddies.'

The three Infants nodded solemnly. Then the headteacher, Mr Gibson, walked into the hall.

'Quiet, please, children. Now, I hope you've had a good party. But before you go home, there's a lovely surprise for you all. Can you guess who's come to our school this afternoon? He's come all the way from Lapland and he's carrying a great big sack.'

'Father Christmas!'

'It's Santa Claus!'

'I reckon we'll get presents!'

'It's him! He's come! He's come!'

Jenny and Jodie were shouting too. Rebecca looked up, but remained silent.

And then the man – the wrong man – walked into the hall.

Even the grown-ups were astounded. There was obviously some mistake. The stranger himself stood in the doorway, looking as surprised as anyone. His hair was thick and as white as snow, but he didn't even wear a hood. Though his face seemed reddened by the cold weather, his beard was clipped far too short. Nobody spoke. During the silence, he glanced nervously around him.

Keith Wilson – a five-year-old from Mrs Hurn's class – noticed that the man carried no sack, burst into tears, kicked his heels and said that he wanted to go home.

'Can I ... Oh dear! Can I help you?' the headteacher faltered.

A bright red sweater and a pair of jeans was all the man offered for costume.

Then he answered with a nervous smile and a sudden burst of words. His voice was high and dry; his speech full of trilling r's, stretched vowels and clicking consonants.

'Uh'm no frome yuer perts, bu' uh naw thet's tame to fetch the bairns.'

Mr Gibson said, 'Thank you very much. If you'd like to wait a minute, we'll do our best to help you.'

The stranger stood to the side and everyone gasped with relief as another figure passed into the hall. This second man pulled no surprises. He wore a long, hooded gown. His boots were large and black, with the proper fur trimmings. The beard on his face was so bushy, you could hardly see his mouth. Most important of all, he carried an enormous sack over his shoulder. Little Keith Wilson stopped crying.

With one mind, forty Infants jumped up and rushed across the hall to meet him.

'Rather unfortunate timing!' Mrs Rudge muttered. Then, noticing the three girls who still sat at their table, she walked over to them.

'Are you sure you're not going to be sick, Rebecca?' she asked.

Rebecca shook her head.

'Well, why don't you go and meet Santa Claus?'

Rebecca said she'd go in a minute.

'And you two? Don't say you're poorly as well!'

'We're looking after Rebecca, Miss,' Jenny explained.

No sooner had Mrs Rudge gone than the girls were chatting again. None of them mentioned dogs or tortoises or even hivermation.

But Jenny said how all that Father Christmas stuff was also sort of fibbing.

'You see, Rebecca – when you go to Home Stores, Father Christmas is fat. But if you nip over to Woolworths, he's there too and, what's more, he's gone all thin!'

'Reckon Jenny got to be right,' added the other twin.

Jenny was in no two minds about it.

'We went shopping in Ipswich once and there was this

Father Christmas standing by the toy bit in Debenhams and he goes, "Yo ho ho, little girl – and what's your name?" So I go, "Jenny Wright and I want a Silkygirl Doll or else a Golden Stars Pony," since me and Jodie and Mum tried everywhere for 'em and we reckoned they were all sold out. After that – don't you remember, Jodie? – you had to go to the loo and Mum got all riled 'cos there was a long queue. And then we saw Father Christmas come out of the men's toilets and I don't think that's right. Do you?'

'What?'

'Well, Rebecca, I don't think the real Father Christmas would ... you know,' Jenny whispered. 'Go to the loo.'

Rebecca had never thought about this before.

'Our mum says there's the real Father Christmas and there's his helpers too.'

'Yip,' agreed Jodie.

'Come on, then,' Jenny suddenly shouted. 'Come on then, or we'll miss him!'

Whether this was the real Father Christmas or a mere helper, the twins seemed no longer to care. They raced across the hall to join the queue for presents. Rebecca followed more calmly behind them. They were all given long, flat parcels that contained felt-tip pens. By the time the twins had ripped theirs open, Rebecca had gone.

Unnoticed now, the strange man in the red sweater had moved over to the PE apparatus. He leant against the vaulting box that could only be used by Juniors. For a moment or two he did not see the redheaded girl in front of him.

Nor did he know what to answer when she spoke.

'I think you're the real one!' she said. 'The real Christmas man!'

His mouth hung open and he cocked his head to one side as if he had not heard her properly.

'Och, muh wee lassie, ud ne'er hewdwink a bairn! Uh've

69

come tay fetch muh grandson – Gregory. Uh'm no' a real
Father Christmas . . .'

Rebecca hardly understood a word. Not that this shook
her faith for one second. On the contrary, you would not
expect a real Christmas man to speak in normal English.
Helpers did. Of course they did! Most of them came from
big shops in Ipswich. This man was different. He even
sounded right. He was speaking in Claus talk or Lappish.

He would have moved away. But the eyes of the tiny,
redheaded girl glistened: she looked as if she might cry.
Suddenly she blurted out the story of her tortoise. The
straw-filled box in the cold shed. Her father's talk of a
long, long sleep. Her fears that the pet was slowly cooling
down and that soon he'd be completely cold, which meant
he would be dead.

The man from the north found it hard to follow her. He
put a hand on her trembling shoulder and muttered
something in Lappish. Rebecca failed to understand. But
now was her last chance.

'Will you?' she said. 'Will you please bring me one? Will

70

you bring me a tortoise for Christmas?'

The Christmas man stared at her, completely perplexed.

'Please?'

His eyes suddenly sparkled. He nodded. He must have understood!

'Well, maybe thar's tame to make one o' wewd?'

'Wewd?'

'Ay, o' wewd. A model o' wewd!'

'A model?'

'Ay, lassie.'

The girl hesitated.

'Yes. Oh yes!' she called out. 'But can you make it so it will move?'

The real man raised his eyebrows. Once again he laughed and nodded.

'Whar's yuh hoos?' he asked.

She told him she lived in the white house on the hill. That would be enough. If he was the real man, he would find it.

Suddenly parents were coming into the hall, looking for their children and chatting with the teachers. The head-teacher had returned to find the stranger.

'I understand you're related to Gregory Stuart and you've come down south for Christmas.'

The bearded man smiled and muttered a few Lappish words.

Then, before she knew it, Rebecca's mother stood by her. Mrs Rudge also joined them, explaining that Rebecca seemed very quiet.

'Tired, I expect,' Mrs Starling answered, 'and no doubt over-excited.'

Even Santa Claus had left the hall by now. Rebecca wondered if he had gone back to his job at Debenhams. The real Christmas man walked off with the headteacher.

71

She realized she had not even said goodbye to him.

But she felt something glow deep inside her as she fetched her coat from the classroom.

She felt the same glow every step of the way, as they walked up the hill towards home.

During the week between the end of term and Christmas Eve, Rebecca had not seen much of her father. But she was quite used to this. Mr Starling returned late in the evenings. Even if Rebecca were still up, he was often too tired to talk.

'I spend most of my working life controlling people's sleep,' he complained. 'When I get home I'm so exhausted I can't keep awake myself!'

His wife laughed. She knew he liked his job. Anaesthetists were important people. Putting patients to sleep for operations, monitoring their heartbeats, finally bringing them safely back to wakefulness. Christmas was always busy. In the last week before the holiday, the surgeons liked to complete the routine operations. That way, Christmas itself was clear, except for emergencies.

'Rebecca all right?' he yawned, as he climbed into bed alongside his wife.

'Sort of. But she seems to have formed some very odd ideas!'

'Probably thinking of Father Christmas!'

'Yes. That's just it. Tonight I said that Santa Claus was coming and she said: "Yes, and so's the other Christmas man, and soon the tortoise will be moving."'

Mr Starling, who had explained about the sleeping tortoise time and time again, made no comment.

'I think I'll give her a goodnight kiss,' he muttered a moment later.

'I wouldn't do that, Robert. You'll only wake her up. If

72

you must go, just poke your head round the door.'

'Don't worry. I'll be as quiet as a mouse.'

Mr Starling left the bed and plodded across the landing like a drugged elephant. He peered into his daughter's bedroom. In the glow of the night-light she appeared to sleep peacefully, her red hair spread across the pillow and her mouth slightly open.

He was surprised to find that, by the time he returned to their room, his wife had switched off her reading lamp. Climbing into bed, he leant over to kiss her.

''Night, Sue.'

Her mouth was slightly open too.

''Night,' she mumbled. It was more like a sigh than a word. She had been busy preparing everything for Christmas Day. Granny Starling was coming over from Woodbridge first thing in the morning. No wonder she was tired out. She would need all the rest she could get.

Before Mr Starling could fall asleep himself, the central heating went off. He knew this because of the clicks from the radiator. Then the metal cooled completely and the pipes stopped vibrating.

A minute later he was staring at the luminous dials of the old-fashioned alarm-clock. Ten thirty-five. He couldn't relax. Maybe it was the stress of work. Six operations in one day! Every time he closed his eyes, he saw a small screen and the fluctuating line of a patient's heartbeat.

'You awake?' he whispered to his wife.

No answer.

He rolled over and closed his eyes again. Something fell from the end of the bed and hit the floor with a clonk.

As soon as he realized he'd have to get up, he felt incredibly sleepy. He slid from the blankets and, groping round to the end of the bed, trod on something round and

73

soft. Whatever it was, he had squelched it flat. Suddenly there was a pungent smell of juice in the room. When he bent down, he realized he had trodden on a tangerine.

The next mystery object was a carrier bag. He put a hand inside it: it was full of items for a stocking.

So Father Christmas had slipped up! Left the presents on the wrong bed!

No doubt Father Christmas was very tired too.

'Sue! Sue!' he whispered.

His wife was fast asleep.

Deciding to complete Santa's work himself, Mr Starling made his way to the bathroom and switched on the shaving light. He dumped the squashed tangerine into the basin and examined a few items from the bag. The first was a box of wine gums. Then came a miniature doll's dress and a pencil-sharpener shaped like a pink pig. He had seen enough. Placing the bag on the dirty-clothes' basket, he crept into his daughter's room in search of the empty stocking.

Rebecca was sitting bolt-upright in bed, firmly clutching it.

'Is that him, Daddy? I heard a bump. Is that him, Daddy? Didn't he come?'

'No, no,' the father whispered. 'Lie down, Rebecca. Shut your eyes and snuggle down. He never comes to children who aren't sleeping. You know that.'

Rebecca lay down again and screwed her eyes up ridiculously tight.

Mr Starling took the bag back to the bedroom and waited another ten minutes. Before attempting to complete Santa's work, he peered into Rebecca's room.

'Why not?' she said.

'What do you mean? And why aren't you asleep?'

'Why aren't you supposed to see him?'

Mr Starling yawned.

'You're not supposed to see him, because if you did, there wouldn't be any surprise when you woke up on Christmas morning.'

'But I already did see him.'

'You mean at school?'

'Yes – and at Debenhams and at Woolworths and out-side the Town Hall and when the Christmas sleigh drove round Brayford and when ...'

'All right, Rebecca. Point taken. Look, for Pete's sake, if you won't go to sleep for Father Christmas, will you please go to sleep for me?'

She smiled at him. He bent to kiss her.

'Daddy?'

'Yes, Rebecca.'

'Do you think Thomas the Second would wake up if he knew Granny was coming?'

'I am not going to go through all that again. Now, just calm down and go to sleep. Thomas is hibernating.'

'Why?'

'Because he doesn't like the cold.'

'But I don't like the cold and I'm not hivermating.'

Mr Starling grunted. At that moment, human hiber-nation was a very attractive proposition.

'Please, Rebecca – please go to sleep!'

He turned towards the door.

'Daddy?'

'Rebecca! I've had just about enough!'

Her face fell. Mr Starling had raised his voice harshly. It was hard to be firm at Christmas time.

'Well?'

'I want to whisper ... I want to whisper you something.'

'Well, whisper it quickly then!'

'There's more than one, Daddy!'

'More than one what?'

The girl whispered even more quietly: 'More than one Christmas man!'

'Yes, Rebecca. Father Christmas has helpers!'

'I know. But there's not just the helpers, Daddy. I met the other Christmas man.'

'Yes, Rebecca. I'm sure you did . . .'

'You don't believe in the other man, do you? But you'll see. You'll see in the morning! He'll bring me a moving tortoise. You'll see him move in the morning!'

Mr Starling could recall seeing no toy tortoise in the carrier bag. But it was too late to worry about details.

Doubt must have shown on his face.

'I know you don't believe in him, Daddy. But you'll see in the morning.'

As soon as he climbed back into bed, Mr Starling was threatened by sleep. He thought he could hold out till eleven-fifteen. He had to.

In fact he dozed off – then woke with a jolt. He could have sworn he heard people singing.

He checked the clock once more. It was all very odd. Too early for midnight mass: too late for carol-singing. Yet the voices were there all right. It was hard to recognize the tune. More like fragments of a carol, really – as if only notes of higher pitch could travel up through the cold night air to the house on the hill above Brayford. He sat up in bed and imagined the singers, half a mile below.

At first he was grateful to them. It was time to fill the stocking.

Third time lucky. She slept like an angel. Soon his work was done. He stopped for a second, wanting to kiss his daughter – but silently left the room.

It was all the more annoying that the singing grew

76

louder. He could now recognize the tune perfectly well. They would wake Rebecca if they came any closer!

Hark! The herald angels sing
Glory to the new-born King . . .

It couldn't be children. Not at this hour. Anyhow, he could now hear bass voices beneath the clear treble.

Joyful all ye nations rise
Join the triumph of the skies . . .

Perhaps they weren't villagers at all, but people from Ipswich who'd visited the Crown and Anchor and were now setting out on the long walk home. Soon they'd be passing the house and, if they had any decency, would quieten down.

But the voices only grew in strength and three minutes later – he couldn't believe it – they were standing in the front garden.

Silent night, holy night . . .

They sang sweetly. He could have killed them. His wife rolled over in her sleep. The singers continued. What could he do but go down and open the door to them?

Standing in his dressing-gown, he was too tired to smile.

'We're collecting for Cancer Research,' someone said, when the last verse was sung.

Mr Starling went back into the house to fetch a pound coin.

'Thank you,' they said. 'And a Merry Christmas!'

'Thank you.'

'Goodnight – and thank you.'

Mr Starling saw them turn to leave. He closed the door a moment too early to see one singer return . . .

The man wore a duffle-coat over his red sweater; a

77

woollen hat covered his white hair. He bent down to place a small box inside the porch and swiftly rejoined the other singers.

Mr Starling had to smile as he crawled back into bed. All that nonsense about Santa's helpers. Poor kids! Everywhere you looked they came in droves – fat ones, short ones, tall ones, thin ones. And to top it all, his own daughter had to dream up another man – the *real* one, the real Christmas man. A tortoise that would move in the morning, indeed!

In this house, there was only one Christmas man!

At nine o'clock on Christmas Day, the doorbell rang.

Granny, having found a small box in the porch, now held it in her gloved hand. Puzzled, she rang the doorbell a second time.

It was opened by her five-year-old granddaughter.

'Hello, Rebecca. Where's Mummy and Daddy?'

Rebecca explained that they were both tired – so tired that they were still in bed.

'Heavens! You mean they're still asleep at nine o'clock on Christmas Day!'

'Yes.'

'And what have have you been up to?'

'I've been sleeping too.'

They hugged each other and giggled together like old partners in mischief. Then Granny noticed that the girl was holding a stocking.

'I'm so glad I got here early!' she said. 'Come on! We'll unpack it together!'

'What's in that box, Granny?'

'I've no idea. Let's have a look.'

Granny pulled out a small wooden tortoise, attached to a length of string.

'An extra present!' she laughed.

'Yes, Granny – an extra present. It came from the real Christmas man.'

The elderly woman was already down on all fours, pulling the tortoise behind her along the length of the hall.

'*You* believe me, don't you, Granny!'

'Yes, of course I do!' Granny Starling replied, without hesitation. 'Now, pass me another wine gum – a black one, please.'

'And it does move, doesn't it!'

'Yes, of course it moves! It moves beautifully.'

Granny was right. As Rebecca took a turn at pulling the toy, some device connected to the wheels made the head nod from side to side. Left slowly. Right slowly. Perfect. Reptilian.

Rebecca's father had dressed quickly. Maybe he was only half awake when he finally appeared.

'Hello, Mum. Aren't you going to take off your coat? I expect you'd like some coffee.'

He didn't seem to notice the tortoise. Not, that is, till he trod on it with a howl of astonishment. Passing Granny Starling in the arabesque position, he pirouetted into the wall, bounced off it, recovered his balance, lost it again – and landed on his bottom.

Christmas Day went with a swing – or, in Mr Starling's case, with a slight limp.

'I can't understand where the toy came from,' he kept muttering. Like the children of Brayford Primary School, he was beginning to find more than one Father Christmas very muddling.

'You have to admit, it's very well made!' Granny Starling insisted. 'Quite like the toys I used to have when I was a little girl. Safe, solid, reliable toys. It didn't break – even under your weight, Robert. Clever – but simple and strong!'

Granny Starling was right: the tortoise hadn't been damaged at all. Rebecca played with it constantly until the Spring.

Granny and Gretel

'I know! Granny can be the witch!' Rebecca suddenly shouted. 'I'm Gretel and Daddy's Hansel. So you've got to go into The Grove first, Granny. And when you've found the fallen-down tree, then you have to pretend it's your gingerbread house and then you've got to shout really loud and then Hansel and I will come along and ...'

'Rebecca! Don't you think you're being a bit bossy?' interrupted Mr Starling. His own mother, Granny Starling, was looking rather tired. After all, she was sixty-five years old. They had taken the Ipswich Road towards Brayford, turned off to follow a path up to the Top Green, walked down to the River Gippen, which they crossed by footbridge, then along the Lower Green to the copse of trees known as The Grove. Even if they took an easier route back, that was a lot for one afternoon.

Gretel lead Granny by the hand.

'You go through there and then, after a bit, you'll get to the fallen tree.'

'Rebecca! Did you hear what I said?'

The redheaded girl, out of breath with excitement, turned towards her father.

'Don't worry, Robert,' Granny said, as she passed through a swing-gate into the woodland. 'We can stay for another five minutes before we go home.'

Granny Starling was laughing. She spoilt her only granddaughter. 'That's what Grannies are for!' she would say. 'That's what Grannies are for!'

Mr Starling watched his mother disappear into the wood, clutching her handbag. He hoped the ground would not be too muddy. Suddenly he felt a hand in his own. His daughter, Rebecca, stared up at him, wide-eyed. She did not speak. She led him through the gate and in amongst the trees.

It was New Year's Day – bright and clear. As they walked on into the depths of the wood, pools of light interrupted the gloom. For the moment the ground was quite firm.

'Hansel! Hansel! Don't cry, Hansel!'

Mr Starling was not crying, he was looking at his watch. A few minutes of make-believe couldn't do any harm.

'But, Gretel! I'm frightened. I think we've lost our way. I'm hungry and soon it will be night time and we've nowhere to sleep.'

He thought he was doing quite well. All the same, he kept his eyes open. If any other people happened to be near ... Well, it would be a bit embarrassing.

'*And so the two children walked deeper into the forest,*' Rebecca narrated solemnly. Her parents had read the storybook to her dozens and dozens of times. She could repeat it now, almost word for word. '*But after a while they grew so tired that they could walk no further ...*'

'Hansel, tonight we shall have to sleep by that tree. Hurry, dear brother of mine.'

'Don't you dare lie down, Rebecca! You'll get your coat filthy,' said her father.

So the two of them just crouched down by the roots of an oak. They shut their eyes for about ten seconds and, when they opened them again, pretended it was morning.

'Did you sleep well, Hansel?'

'Very well, Gretel. What's for breakfast?'

'There's nothing to eat, dear brother. Nothing! We'll just have to walk through the forest. Maybe we will come upon a nice little cottage where we could find food and shelter.'

Mr Starling glanced at his watch. He was beginning to wonder where Granny had gone. Soon they came to the fallen log. But of course, the witch was not meant to be at home! He'd forgotten that detail of the story.

'Look! Look! A gingerbread house!'

Hansel and Gretel approached the log cautiously. Then Gretel broke off a piece of imagined wall and passed it to her brother.

'Um! Thank you,' Mr Starling said. 'That *is* delicious!'

Suddenly he heard someone approach. It wasn't the witch, but a rather over-weight, middle-aged man who sweated along in a red tracksuit.

Pretending he had not been eating gingerbread at all, Mr Starling reddened and thrust his hands into his pockets. Gretel was eating a chocolate windowsill.

'Hello, Robert,' the runner gasped.

It was Mr Warder from the Gippen Estate. As soon as he had panted out of sight, Mr Starling slipped back into the part of Hansel. He felt less comfortable this time.

Just as Gretel reached up to pull off a lump of marzipan roof, they heard a blood-curdling whine.

'Hello, my little pretties! So you like to eat my house. Eat up, my scrumptious children. Gobble all you will. In fact, why don't you step inside?'

The witch had jumped out from behind a bush. (Mr Starling wondered where she had left her handbag, but pushed the thought from his mind.)

Actually she was doing very well. Suddenly he thought back to his own childhood in Woodbridge. Thirty years ago. Almost half a lifetime. Yet the small things, even now, he recalled so clearly. The swing that his father had made and hung from the bough of the oak. Granny, his own mother, reading folk-tales in his bedroom. Her voice. The weight of her body as she sat on the edge of his bed.

Her hair, then as red as Rebecca's but now turned silvery, fell over her forehead as she acted out her part. She brushed it back impatiently.

So much had changed. She was widowed now, and elderly. So much had changed and yet ... 'Step inside, my little dainties! Step inside and gorge yourselves!'

The voice, even now, sent a delicious chill down his spine. Hand in hand with Gretel, he stepped into the house. Before long he found himself trapped in a cage. Invisible bars hemmed him in. Gretel wept and wailed for her brother, but already the witch had turned the key, cackling wickedly.

Supposing John Warder should jog back down the same path? And perhaps there were other neighbours out walking with their families. Crouching in his invisible prison, Mr Starling realized how ridiculous he would look. Granny didn't seem to care. She was too busy collecting faggots of wood and preparing to light her oven. Gretel helped her. She had no choice. As Mr Starling watched them, he couldn't help noticing the same wide-eyed excitement in the elderly woman and the girl. Rebecca had inherited more than her granny's red hair: they also shared the same sense of mischief and magic.

'What on earth are you doing, Gretel?' (His daughter was piling up wood with a will.) 'Surely you're ... Surely you're not on the side of the witch?'

He was genuinely relieved when his daughter ran towards him:

'Don't worry!' she explained impatiently. 'I'm only pretending to help her. Don't you remember the end of the story, Daddy? When the witch has lit the oven, she's got to open the cage. Then – just when she's about to put you in – we tell her to lean through the oven door to see if it's really hot enough. And then we have to push her in and she's burnt to a frazzle and we escape and she's never seen again!'

Mr Starling nodded.

His daughter tossed back her red curls and went back to fire-building.

'That's all right, then,' he said.

There was a slight delay when two cocker spaniels sauntered past. Mr Starling stood up straight, despite the bars of the cage, brushed some leaves from his coat and waited. Rebecca insisted they weren't dogs at all, but a pack of ravenous wolves. Then the owner appeared: Mr Maddock, who wore a sheepskin coat and ran a butcher's shop on Brayford Main Street. Granny said the wolves must have guessed there would be a roasting. She raised a crooked finger and sent them away with a spell. They ran off with their tongues hanging out and disappeared after their master.

'All is prepared,' announced the granny-witch. 'Come on, Gretel. You open up the oven door while I fetch your fat little brother. Hurry, child! Hurry! Or I shall turn you into a crusty old toad. Hurry! Hurry! I'm starving!'

She turned the key and pulled back the door of poor Hansel's prison.

'Are you sure the oven is hot enough, Witchy?'

'Why, of course it is, you silly girl.'

'I don't think it is, you know. Why don't you put a finger inside, just to be certain?'

The oven door opened. The witch put a finger in.

'Cats and cauldrons! I'm not so sure!'

'Then why not put your hand in?'

'Bats and blood! The child may be right!'

'Then why not put your arm in?'

'Slugs and slime! I still can't tell!'

'Well, why don't you put your head in?'

As the witch peered inside, Hansel and Gretel pushed with all their might. With a blood-curdling scream, the woman lurched forward. The girl jumped up and down, tugging her father round and round in a dance of relief and triumph.

Granny stood up too, laughing just as triumphantly. Rebecca hugged her. The story was over.

No pools of light broke the gloom now. Mr Starling said it was nearly four o'clock and high time they went home.

They were just passing through the swing-gate when Granny remembered her handbag. She had left it on a tree stump, quite close to a bush.

'Well, we'll have to go back for it,' said Mr Starling. His mother was looking tired by now. She could wait by the gate while he fetched the bag. The problem was, which bush did she mean?

'The one I jumped out from.'

'On the left or the right?'

Granny said it was on the right. But there were several bushes and half a dozen tree stumps.

She had thirty pounds in her handbag as well as her driving licence, her cheque book and banker's card.

'I know which tree stump!' Rebecca declared.

'Then you come with me. Will you be all right, Mother? We'll only be ten minutes. You have a rest. You just wait for us here.'

The father and daughter walked swiftly back to the scene of the play. It was too cold to dawdle and they were anxious about the bag. Even Rebecca remained quiet. The light was so poor that they had to concentrate. Even so, their feet caught against broken branches. The ground which had seemed firm and even in daylight now rose and fell unexpectedly. They were glad to arrive back at the spot. Rebecca disappeared behind Granny's bush and stepped out again, proudly swinging the bag.

Mr Starling thought it would be safer if he carried it. He took it from his daughter and, holding it by the clasp, strode along as manfully as he could.

They had not walked for more than a minute, when Rebecca said, 'Do you remember what happens next?'

Mr Starling looked puzzled.

'Yes, Rebecca. Next we go back to the gate and take Granny home. She's had quite enough for one afternoon.'

'No, no. I mean in the story.'

'The story is over,' he replied firmly. His foot catching in a hidden root, he tripped and nearly dropped the hand-bag. He recovered himself.

'Don't you remember? The story ended when we pushed poor Granny into the oven,' he said.

'No, it didn't.'

'Rebecca, it's late.'

'We still haven't done the going-home bit.'

'Ah! You mean it's time to go back to our house and then Granny can have some tea before she drives back to Woodbridge.'

'No, Daddy. We burnt Granny.'

'Rebecca! Enough is enough!'

'But, Daddy! Daddy! Don't you remember? After we burnt her, we found pots and pots of gold. Come on! We can pretend Granny's handbag is full of gold! And now we have to run all the way back to our house on the edge of the forest. And when we get there . . .'

'Rebecca! That will do!'

'When we get there, our cruel stepmother has died and we give the gold to our father – the woodcutter. He has to hug us and then we live happily ever after.'

'Rebecca! Don't run ahead. You stay with me, do you hear? It's dark. Supposing you lose your way!'

The girl stopped and waited for her father to catch up.

'I know! Granny can be the woodcutter. She can hug us when we arrive.'

Mr Starling laughed a little nervously. His own daughter amazed him. For days and days she would be quiet – almost sullen. Then, without warning, she burst into life, fabricating Father Christmases, reliving fairy stories, inventing parts for herself and for everybody else to play. Granny Starling was almost as bad – worse, when you considered her age.

'Hurry, Hansel – dear brother of mine. Hurry! The forest is full of fierce wolves and soon it will be night!'

'Rebecca! If you run, you'll trip.'

But the girl had already bounded ahead, disappearing around a bend in the path.

'Rebecca! Rebecca!'

He caught sight of her again. But a third time she ran on.

'Rebecca!'

Lost among shadows this time.

'Rebecca!' he shouted angrily. When she reappeared, he would tell her off very sharply.

But Mr Starling saw her no more. Increasing his speed, he came to a fork in the pathway. He had not even noticed it before. Left or right? He was not sure himself.

'Rebecca! Rebecca! Can you hear me?'

From the dark wood ahead – no answer.

Realizing he would have to choose one path or the

other, the father branched off to the right. He felt an onrush of panic. Maybe he would see her in a moment or two. He imagined her running back to him. He wanted to clasp her, to shake her in anger, to hold her tiny body against his own till her crying ceased and they could walk back to Granny, her hand in his. But still he did not see her. This ridiculous handbag! He could have hurled it, with all its treasures, into the darkness of the wood. He would have hurled any riches away for sight or sound of his daughter.

Instead, he sprinted on. He had been right in his choice of pathway and soon saw the silhouette of his mother on the far side of the gate.

'Rebecca! Where's Rebecca!' he pleaded.

'With you, Robert! What on earth do you mean?'

'But she's not with me. She ran ahead. I tried to stop her. I tried, but she just wouldn't listen!'

'Oh heavens, Robert! Surely, you couldn't have . . .'

But there was no point in arguing. Robert Starling passed the bag back to his mother.

'Oh Robert! It's dark and cold. She'll be terrified. If only I hadn't been so stupid and left the bag behind!'

'You stay here. Just stay on this spot. She may find her way to the gate.'

He wanted to tell his mother it wasn't her fault. It was Rebecca's own stupid fault – and his. But what was the point of laying blame. That could come later – when she was found. If she was found. If she was found!

'You stay here!' he said. 'I'm going back again.'

But before he could leave, he saw a strange figure jogging heavily towards them. Far too large to raise any hopes, he stopped by the swing-gate, breathing heavily.

'Hello, Robert.'

It was John Warder in his red tracksuit.

'What's up? Can I help?'

'We've lost Rebecca. You didn't see her? You must have seen something!'

'Not a soul. What do you mean? You've lost her?'

'She ran off in the wood.'

'Come on, then. She can't have got very far.'

Mr Warder seemed quite calm in the circumstances. Maybe he wouldn't have sounded so calm if the lost child had been his own.

They ran back to the fork in the path – Robert Starling sweating with fear, John Warder with exhaustion.

'Which way now? asked John.

'Oh God! You try the other path. I'll go back to the fallen log where ...'

Both of them left, stumbling in their haste. Before a minute was up, Mr Starling heard a strange panting. Some animal. No – several animals. They were suddenly brushing against his legs. One of them licked his hand and they disappeared again. They seemed to have run off in the direction of the log.

'Oh, no! It just can't be true!' muttered Rebecca's father. 'Please, God! It can't be true! This isn't really happening.'

'They can be the fierce wolves, Daddy,' he remembered Rebecca saying.

Then he saw a torch – just a thin point of light. It flickered and wobbled, disappeared and shone again. As Mr Starling approached it, he heard the voice of a man ...

'Well, you can't stay here all night, can you? You'll die of cold! You can't just stand here. I know you've been told not to go with strangers, but I'm not really a stranger, am I? Your Mum bought a leg of lamb from me last week. And don't you remember your Christmas turkey? Well ... Oh, come on, now. No good upsetting yourself!'

The butcher spoke gently, but it was no use. Above his coaxing voice rose the thin wail of the terrified girl.

'I want my daddy!'

'I know, dear. But unless you ...'

'Daddy! Daddy! I want my daddy!'

The torch's beam was suddenly turned towards the approaching man.

Rebecca gave a long sob and ran to her father's arms.

When they arrived back at the swing-gate, Granny Starling hugged Rebecca too.

Only the cocker spaniels seemed unconcerned. Mr Maddock called them to heel and, saying he was glad that all had ended well, set off briskly across the Lower Green.

John Warder smiled.

'I'd better get back for a bath,' he said, 'before the old muscles stiffen up.'

'Thank you for your help.'

John Warder wobbled into action and panted off. A moment later the darkness engulfed him.

As for the Starlings, they had not even passed the horse-chestnut trees when Rebecca began crying again. Her father held her right hand, Granny held the left. Between them, her thin body was convulsed by sobbing. No one spoke. There was nothing to be said. Then they crossed the Ipswich Road, reaching the pavement that led up the hill to the house where a warm bed was waiting. They crossed the road bridge over the Gippen. Even now, the girl was still crying.

'Come on, dear. It's not the end of the world!' said Granny. 'Let's walk faster. It'll warm us up.'

'I feel such a fool,' her son muttered.

'Don't be silly, Robert.'

'But I do.'

'Well, you shouldn't. Every parent loses their child. Just once. It's awful. For a moment you think you'll die of worry. But it happens, Robert. It happens. Maybe it has to happen.'

Robert Starling did not reply. He walked sullenly as the hill grew steeper, now shouldering all the blame.

'Heavens, Robert! Do you think you're the first person ever to lose a child?'

They came to the last street lamp in Brayford. By its light he saw his mother smiling.

'I lost you!' she said. 'I'll never forget it. You were only four at the time.'

Mr Starling glanced at his mother again. She giggled. She actually managed to giggle, after all that had happened!

'You won't remember it, Robert. But I do. It's silly, really, but I never told a soul about it – not even your father.'

Mr Starling didn't feel like a story. But his mother had

waited by the gate so calmly. She was tired and cold. Half an hour she had waited and worried by that gate – and not once complained.

'Go on,' he said, half listening.

'Well, I used to take you to the park down by the River Deben, almost every afternoon. One day I thought we might take a different route home. So, instead of following the river back to the town, we began to climb Badger's Hill, which used to be all woodland.'

Granny stopped, as if so many details had rushed into her mind that she could not keep track of them.

But at least Rebecca had stopped as well. At least she had stopped crying.

'Granny?'

'Yes, Rebecca?'

'Did Daddy run ahead?'

'Oh yes. That's just it. All the way up the hill he kept hiding behind trees and jumping out to frighten me.'

'And were you frightened?'

'Terrified.'

'But when were you most frightened, Granny?'

'Oh, the most frightened I ever was – that's easy. The most frightened, without a doubt, was when he *didn't* jump out. And there I was at the top of the hill, looking behind every bush and tree.'

'Go on, Granny. What happened next?'

'What happened next? I panicked. I ran down the far side of the hill shouting, "Robert! Robert! Robert!" When I reached the botton, I still hadn't found him. It must have been spring or summer. I remember a man cutting a hedge. He put down his clippers and helped me to search. Then a lady came along. Very bossy, she was. She kept saying careless people like me didn't deserve to have children. Suddenly I remembered the main road. I ran on as fast as I could, praying he hadn't reached it. Past some cottages. Past some allotments. Suddenly I heard him crying, "Mummy! Mummy!" I turned round to look at the vegetable patches and out popped his head from a row of runner beans.'

Before they knew it they had walked the last half-mile and entered the house.

Rebecca's mother had done her share of worrying, wondering where they were. At first she seemed cross with her husband. But after all, these things happened. They were bound to happen once.

After a hot bath, Rebecca came downstairs in her dressing-gown. Her mother gave her baked beans on toast.

'Can I play with my toy tortoise?' she asked, as soon as she had finished.

She pulled it up and down the living room for a few minutes; but Granny did not join in.

'I ought to go home,' she said.

'Can't you stay just one more day?' Rebecca begged.

'Certainly not? Your father is going to be very busy at work and your mother must be exhausted. Anyhow, I should think they've had quite enough of Granny by now.'

'No, they haven't.'

'Yes, they have.'

'Well, *I'm* still on holiday.'

'I know, but ...'

'And tomorrow morning we could do another play, Granny!'

'Not Hansel and Gretel, I hope!'

'No! No! No! We could do a play about Daddy in Woodbridge, when he was a little boy. I can be Daddy and you can be the bossy lady and Mummy could be you when you took him for a walk, and Daddy can be the man who was clipping the hedge, or – if you want – you could be the mummy and Mummy can clip the hedge 'cos sometimes ladies do clip hedges and . . .'

'Rebecca, don't leave that wooden tortoise in the hallway. And it's time you were off to bed.'

'But, Daddy!'

'We'll let Granny get off home right away. Just for once, we'll let Granny be Granny.'

Mr Sheen's Classic Vienna Regulator

It had all started one Saturday afternoon back in October. As far as Brenton Sheen was concerned, it wasn't funny.

Clock mania, they called it. It was like a disease. Mr Sheen had been perfectly well when they left Brayford. Maybe it was Sylvia Sheen's fault. After all, she was the one who'd suggested a visit to the Clock Museum at Bury St Edmunds. Then again, how was she to know? How could anybody have guessed what an hour amongst the timepieces would do to her husband, Guy? An hour. That was all it needed. By the time they stepped out of the museum and on to the pavement of Angel Hill, the virus had already entered his system.

'It's your birthday in three weeks' time, dear, isn't it?' Mr Sheen said. 'How would you like a clock?'

Brenton had seen straight away that his mother was delighted. Ever since they had moved to Riverview – the most expensive property on the Gippen Estate – she had felt the hallway needed something. A barometer would have done; a clock would be even better.

'Oh, Guy! What a lovely idea!' she cried out, her face radiant in the October sunlight. 'There are some beautiful clocks at Denton's in Ipswich. Perhaps we could . . .'

Mr Sheen had looked at her, puzzled and offended.

'I wasn't intending to buy you a clock.'

'Oh!'

'It is my intention to make you one.'

Even Brenton had been surprised. The glint of pride in his father's eyes was very disturbing.

All in all, he was quite a practical man. The previous year he had assembled a greenhouse. He could also service the car. He had tiled the bathroom with no problem and plumbed a dishwasher into the kitchen. But Brenton couldn't help thinking that the art of clockmaking was quite another thing.

'Denton's are giving fifteen per cent discounts as an autumn offer,' his mother announced that evening.

Mr Sheen did not answer. For although clock mania was in its first stages, it had already affected his hearing.

Odd things began to happen at Riverview. For instance, heavy rectangular parcels would be delivered by the postman almost every morning. At breakfast, Mr Sheen would no longer read the newspaper. Instead he would rip the packages open, poring over their contents and forgetting to finish his cereal like an over-excited child.

ENGLISH LONGCASE CLOCKS FOR THE MODERN MAKER and A BEGINNER'S GUIDE TO BRACKET CLOCK CONSTRUCTION were the first to arrive. These were closely followed by another volume – THE WATCH AND CLOCKMAKER'S HANDBOOK. After the books came magazines, leaflets, plans, catalogues and price lists. For the first time in his life, Mr Sheen was almost always late for work. Each morning his wife would have to push him through the door, before returning to tidy the house. Every shelf, every chair and table seemed covered with words, numbers, photographs and drawings – all of them connected with clocks.

Mother and son coped reasonably well with all this during the early stage of the illness. Most difficult of all were Mr Sheen's long periods of silence. Even on November

17th – Sylvia Sheen's birthday – he hardly spoke. Just a few words, as he presented her with a box of luxury soap. They noticed that 'the clock I'm going to make you for your birthday' had suddenly become 'the clock I'm going to make you for Christmas'. Fine. Sylvia Sheen and Brenton accepted all this. It was only slowly that they realized the disease was moving into a second phase. Mr Sheen became quite jovial. He also became talkative. This was the real trouble. The words had moved from the printed pages into his head and now he began to bandy them about the house. His wife and son feared for his state of mind. One thing was certain, Mr Sheen was now quite incapable of talking normal English.

'Dad! Dad! Did you know Ipswich are playing Liverpool at home tomorrow?' asked Brenton. 'Why don't we go for once, Dad? It should be a good game.'

'The thing about the dead-beat escape wheel system,' Mr Sheen muttered, 'is that, unlike your ordinary anchor escapement, it ensures that the second hand stops dead at every tick. No recoil: more precision. That's what it's all about, you see. Precision, Brenton. Precision.'

Mrs Sheen fared no better. Forgetting herself one evening, she asked him how he had got on at the office.

'Office?' he mumbled, as if she were completely out of her senses.

'Yes, Guy. You remember. The office where you work. Business! Insurance!'

'Fine, Sylvia. Fine. But the problem with pivots is that they have to carry the whole strain of the power-source. Doesn't matter if we're dealing with a weight or spring system.'

Words. Words. Words.

Term ended. December 25th approached. 'The clock I'm going to make you for Christmas' became 'the clock

I'm going to make you for our wedding anniversary'.

And yet more words. They certainly ruined the festivities at Riverview. Instead of talk about decorations, crackers, presents and the turkey, the house was full of clockmaker's jargon. Every second word was pillar or pendulum, bob, collet, finial, lenticle or pinion. Horrible words. Nasty long words that snaked into your mind. Little round words that ricocheted around the house like bullets. The stress under which Brenton and his mother lived became almost unbearable. Worst of all, as Brenton realized with horror, the words had wormed their way into his own mind. He found them repeating themselves in his head – wriggling about like tiny creatures that would not die, however hard he tried to destroy them. *Bobs. Cogs. Ratchet. Escape-wheel arbor. Lenticles. Anchor escapements.* He would try to read or to play with the home-computer, go for a walk or watch TV: it made no difference. The words were there when he went to bed. They were there when he awoke each morning.

When it finally happened, Brenton and his mother could hardly believe it. At precisely three-fifteen on Saturday, January 8th, Mr Sheen burst into the living room and made his announcement.

'The SRE 7!' he shouted.

At first neither mother nor son showed the slightest reaction.

'The SRE 7! I've got it at last. I'll send off an order right away. That's it! The SRE 7!' At the same time he waved a catalogue of replica clocks in front of his wife.

'Here we go again!' Brenton moaned.

He was surprised to see his mother put down her book. She said nothing. Just a hint of a smile came to her lips. Not that she was mocking her husband. Quite the opposite. For the first time in ten weeks he had captured her attention. She reached forward and took the catalogue from him, still open at pages fourteen and fifteen.

'Well, Sylvia? What do you think?'

'This one, Guy?'

'Yes. That's the boy!'

'SRE 7,' she read slowly. 'A Classic Vienna Regulator.' At the same time she held the catalogue up as if, by an act of will, she could transfer the clock from the photograph into real life. Still holding it upward, she walked to the hallway.

'It is rather fetching,' she admitted.

Brenton could not believe it. What was his mother doing? Did she want to encourage him? He walked behind his parents, who were already discussing where the clock might hang to best advantage.

The odd thing was, as he glanced over his mother's shoulder for another look at the catalogue, he suddenly felt as if he had seen the clock before. It was only a feeling. Yet there was something in the shape of the thing – the top section above the dial, in particular . . . Maybe he had seen something like it in the house of a friend or relation. He could not place the memory and the feeling sank away again.

'Here! Just here,' Mrs Sheen concluded. 'It'll be the first thing people see as they step through the door.'

Brenton was furious. His father was laughing triumphantly. Another phase of clock mania had obviously begun. Worst of all, his own mother had caved in. The sickness was contagious. Nobody was safe. All the while, the virus had been working at her system, too. No doubt about it – his mother was clock-struck.

From now on, Brenton realized, he stood alone.

100

Within a week three boxes arrived from J.R.Granville & Sons of Peterborough by special delivery. The largest contained the ninety-four pieces of shaped wood which were to make up the body of the clock. The second package was heavy and compact: Mr Sheen unwrapped it with even greater care till at last he feasted his eyes on the PF 18 Keininger movement. Finally, he came to a long, thin item cased in polystyrene. It was the pendulum with its bob – a disc of white enamel set in brass. Mrs Sheen stood at the kitchen table, cooing with delight as the unpacked treasures were laid out before her.

'Shall we take it up to the room?' she asked, almost as though they were talking about a baby.

'Whose side are you on?' Brenton hissed, walking in disgust to the lounge.

He sat down on the sofa, then stretched out, plonking his feet on the cushions defiantly. It was incredible. His mother and father had already cleared the guest room, moving the spare bed across the landing. 'That'll be lovely for you,' his mother had said. 'When your cousin Ricky comes to stay, he'll be able to sleep in your bedroom with you.' Brenton had not been taken in for a minute. There was nothing lovely about it at all. A portable workbench and an old table had been put there in place of the bed. The plans for the Classic Vienna Regulator were already pinned to the wall. His father had bought a whole range of equipment – tiny pincers and screwdrivers for the movement; clamps, jigs, vices, knives, planes, chisels, mallet and pinhammer for the assembly of the mahogany case. Then, to add insult to injury, Mr Sheen insisted that animal glue of the old-fashioned type was far better than any modern adhesives. And so, each weekend and almost every evening, he would set his glue pot on the gas burner. As a result, the house was infected with a revolting smell –

a sort of fishy odour with a tang of horse manure.

From the moment she had seen the photo of the Classic Vienna Regulator, Mrs Sheen had become a different woman. Time did not improve her condition. While Brenton walked around with a handkerchief pressed against his nose, she busied herself about the house as though the smell of animal glue had, for her, all the fragrance of perfume. Just occasionally she would creep into the spare room – now known as the workshop – and edge up behind her husband. Very quietly. Humbly. As if it would never do to disturb a master craftsman. For the first week or so there was not much to show for all the work. Then, by late January, the frame began to take on the shape of a clock. There was still no clockface and the whole structure was harsh and rectangular. But before they knew it, Mr Sheen had boiled up another disgusting mixture and the pediment was glued into position. Mrs Sheen ran her fingers across it. The pediment had transformed the box into a clock case, just as a roof transforms four walls into a house.

Once more, the feeling that he'd seen it before astounded Brenton. The pediment or roof of the clock was triangular – or it would have been, were it not for the ornaments and mouldings. The sides sloped upward, curved down in two symmetrical loops, then rose again to meet in a point. Brenton knew this shape. It was a local shape. A village shape. He had seen the shape before somewhere, in a dark corner of Brayford.

'It's not halfway finished really,' Mr Sheen explained. 'You wait, Sylvia! You just wait till the mouldings are in place. Right at the top – just here, look – there'll be a brass finial. Look – I'll hold it there, just to give you an idea.'

Lying on his bed, Brenton could hear everything. He

already knew how the brass bobble would look when placed at the top of the pediment. He sulked in silence for another half hour – but at tea he could not keep quiet.

'It's not a real grandfather clock,' he jibed. 'Not my idea of a grandfather clock. A decent grandfather clock's a lot bigger than that. That's more like a sort of dwarf grandfather clock. A baby clock! Won't it look a bit silly, standing out there in the hallway?'

His parents stared at him.

'That's not very polite or kind!' Mrs Sheen said. She made it sound as if he had been rude to a child – a younger brother or sister.

He had been rude. He could not stop himself. His feelings were too strong.

'Actually,' Mr Sheen said with quiet confidence, 'it's not meant to be a longcase clock. It's a Regulator, as well you know, Brenton. A Vienna Regulator, based on an 1873 original. And like all Vienna Regulators, it will hang upon the wall. Two-and-a-half feet of sheer perfection!'

Work progressed steadily over the next weeks. Mr Sheen was determined that all should be finished in time for 19th February. He already talked to friend and stranger alike of 'the clock I'm making my wife for our wedding anniversary'. This time it was really going to happen. All he had to do now was bolt the Kieninger movement on to the backplate, fit the glass door, give the rich mahogany a last polish and finally attach the brass pendulum.

'Mum?' Brenton asked, as they sat alone in the lounge.

'Yes, dear?'

'What can I get you for your wedding anniversary?'

'Don't you worry, dear!'

'I'm not worried. What do you want?'

'Honestly, dear, with a brand new Vienna Regulator, what more could I possibly ask for?'

103

The boy reddened with anger. A brand new regulator! What more could she want? Fine. All right. A replica, built in a spare room. Fine. If that's what she wanted. Fine. That was fine.

Suddenly his anger left him. The strange sensation that he'd seen the clock before flooded back. Where? How? Like a ghost. A ghost-clock. A wish-clock. He could not help it – his imagination ran away with him. Already he pictured the scene on the day of the anniversary. The Vienna Regulator would be hung on the wall. His father would gloat with pride and his mother sigh with satisfaction. But at that moment Brenton would stride in through the front door, another regulator – his regulator – in his arms. Not a replica. Not a copy. 'Here you are, Mum. This is from me.' Only *he* would be holding out the real thing.

Of course it was only wishful thinking. And yet . . . and yet he had seen it somewhere.

In the few days that remained before the anniversary, Brenton mooched around the village as if haunted. As it happened, the school was on half-term holiday. The spare time made things worse.

'Why don't you go for a ride on your racer?' suggested Mrs Sheen.

The boy shook his head.

'Or go over to the Lower Green? I drove past this morning and there must have been twenty children playing football there.'

He shook his head again and walked up to the bathroom. For some reason, Brenton had got into the habit of sitting in there on top of the wicker laundry basket. He was haunted even now by the memory of a clock – a clock that existed somewhere.

'Why wicker?' he would ask himself, like a detective who knew he had found a clue but did not know where it might lead. 'Wickerwork, wickerwork, clockwork, wickerwork,' he intoned, kicking his heels against the base of his perch. 'Wickerwork, clockwork; clockwork, wickerwork . . .' Maybe he was cracking up. But there had to be a connection.

He did not sort it out till Friday, 18th. His mother was watching TV; his father was in the workshop. The smell of glue had now given way to that of furniture polish. Sitting on the laundry basket as usual, Brenton suddenly thought of a wicker chair. He was getting warm. Two wicker chairs. That was warmer still. Yes! Two wicker chairs, one balanced on top of the other. Two old wicker chairs and behind them – just poking out over the top – the pediment of an old Vienna Regulator. An antique. An original. Yes. The real thing!

He ran down the stairs and burst into the living room.

'I'm going out, Mum?'

'Why?'

'Feel like it.'

'Well, really! You be back in twenty minutes. Cold tea at six-thirty. Whatever's got into you?'

He did not answer. A minute later he was on his racer. In the yellow light of the street lamps, he swept round Plover Crescent, turned right into Dunlin Road and pedalled down Main Street like a maniac. He arrived at Weatherby's shop – between the Post Office and the chemist – and flung his bike down on the pavement. Then he remembered the front lamp and bent down to unclip it. Wicker! Wicker chairs! Old furniture! Weatherby! He knew the regulator hung on the end wall, even before he looked.

Brenton was not disappointed. In the beam of his cycle

105

lamp he caught sight of the triangular pediment. He could even see the top half of the white dial, just behind the top chair. There was nothing he could do about it tonight. But he still had Saturday morning to contact Henry Weatherby – and fifteen pounds in his savings box.

All evening he stared at WILSON'S PRICE GUIDE TO WATCHES AND CLOCKS. His father was delighted. A real hobby, he said. Clocks were a delight for life. Brenton smiled back. What he didn't say was that an antique regulator hung on a wall in Brayford. Nor did he betray the slightest surprise that the clock was valued at several hundred pounds.

Henry Weatherby wouldn't have a clue. A nice old boy – but his business was a joke.

He had owned the shop for nearly thirty years and lived in a flat above it. For the last ten years, however, he had not been inside the shop itself. Nobody had been inside it.

They couldn't. There wasn't room. In fact there was only just enough space to open the door. Beyond it, furniture, tools, musical instruments, books, clothes and odd bits of outdated machinery were jammed in together in a compact mess. The shop space – if you could call it space – ran about twenty feet parallel to the pavement. It was scarcely more than ten feet in depth. Everybody knew that Weatherby tended the shop for about an hour each day. But never the same hour. To catch him standing out on the pavement in his old grey cardigan was a matter of good luck and good weather.

When you did see him, he was always armed with a hooked pole. This was used in an occasional attempt to retrieve some distant item. Most of the valuable objects within easy reach had long since been sold. This left a hoard of unobtainable treasures, poking out from the rubbish. Dealers from Ipswich, Bury St Edmunds and Colchester knew about the shop. Occasionally one of them would turn up. 'You see that silver jug?' they might say. 'I'll give you twenty pounds for it, Mr Weatherby.' 'You can have it,' Henry would mumble. 'You can have it for ten – providing I can get to it.' He would then squeeze his thin body through the door, wave his hooked pole in the air above the mess and give up within a minute.

For this reason, Henry Weatherby's business was known in Brayford as 'The Fishing Shop'.

By ten o'clock on the Saturday, Brenton had been standing outside The Fishing Shop for over an hour. The weather was clear but cold: he began to doubt that Weatherby would ever come down from the flat.

Then Mrs Trinder came out of the Post Office.

'Wasting your time,' she said.

Brenton shrugged.

'You got to holler if you want him,' the widow continued. 'You gotta do that 'cos the doorbell bust.'

Brenton shrugged again.

'Customer!' the woman shrieked without warning. 'You got a customer, Henry. So just you git down the stairs before he die o' cold.'

A minute later Henry did. He was wearing his grey cardigan and bedroom slippers. He had not forgotten the pole.

'Yip?' he said.

'That clock at the back, Mr Weatherby . . . Is that clock for sale?'

Henry Weatherby shook his head and tut-tutted.

'I'll give you fifteen pounds for it. Look!' Brenton held the money out in front of the man.

Weatherby showed not the slightest sign of interest, but simply peered into his shop as if estimating a distance.

'That clock is for sale,' he muttered drily. 'But it don't follow anyone can buy it.'

'Supposing I . . .'

'That's way beyond reach, boy.'

'But I could come back this afternoon.'

'Sorry, but that's out of the question. I reckon your best bet is to come back when I'm dead and buried.'

Brenton flinched. He could hardly bear it. A genuine Vienna Regulator! He could have matched his dad's replica with the real thing. Fifteen pounds! It would have been a triumph. And now he could not obtain it.

'It's for my mother,' he said, holding back tears.

'I'm sorry, boy, but that clock'll have to stay put. Tell you what, though. You give me a moment to open the door and I reckon I might git a mantle clock for you. I darn near got it last year!'

'But I'd help you, Mr Weatherby. We could move things together.'

'Move? Move things?' The man was deeply shocked.

'Yes. Well ... Oh no! I've got to have a look!' And before the old man had recovered his wits, Brenton had shot inside. Furious, Weatherby thrust his pole beneath a row of washstands in an attempt to fish out the boy. Too late. Brenton had wriggled away.

'What you bust you'll pay for! Now just you come back here!'

But Brenton had already begun his cramped journey. 'I'll get there! I'll get it!' he kept repeating. 'I've just got to get to it somehow!'

It was like a voyage back in time. He fumbled his way through the bric-à-brac of the seventies and sixties – guitars, radios, black-and-white TV sets and several old Hoovers. After that he had to pass beneath a dining table. He resurfaced only to find his way blocked by a sink unit. Back on all fours, he crawled around this and struggled through a strata from the fifties. Enormous wooden golf clubs, tennis rackets in their heavy frames. He peered ahead. A stuffed curlew stared at him. It tilted against an early wireless on one leg: the other had fallen off. Piles of 78 records and a dressmaker's dummy came next. There were larger items too – an enormous radiogram, a cocktail cabinet and bookcase. These were covered with an assortment from the forties – a helmet; two gas-masks and a ukulele. Poking out amongst all the mess were treasures in silver and ivory, copper, pewter and jade. He did not give any of it his attention. He did not stop, though he sweated with effort, till at last he came to the goal itself. He caught sight of the wicker chairs.

He had made it. He wrestled with one chair, then thrust it to the side.

He was staring at the Vienna Regulator. *H.B.Roberts of Manchester, 1873* it said on the dial.

Before touching it, he stood up to collect himself but could not stop his trembling. He realized that Weatherby had moved along the shopfront and was trying to shout something through the window. What did it matter? Only the genuine Vienna Regulator mattered. Raising his hands, he was thrilled by the feel of the mahogany. He pulled. The screws slid easily from the wall. Brenton was holding the clock in his hands. He had done it. This was the real thing!

Four seconds later there followed a kind of soundless explosion. One moment he held a clock: the next moment it had gone. The case simply disintegrated. He was left with a section of side panel: even that was half-eaten by worms. The rest of the clock had powdered on impact as it fell to The Fishing Shop floor. Gone! Firewood! Less solid than firewood ...

Tears in his eyes, he knelt amongst the remains. The triangular pediment was hardly recognizable. He retrieved its brass bobble and turned it gently between a finger and thumb. Then there was the white dial. That was all that survived from 1873.

Where was the rest of the clock? The pendulum and bob? Where had the movement gone. No arbor. No anchor or dead-beat escapement. No lenticle, collet or pinion. The words swarmed back once again. As he knelt there, they plagued him.

He looked up. Henry Weatherby was still tapping on the window, unaware that his own life was about to change.

It began with a slow creak and ended with a crash, as the Welsh dresser keeled forward. It did not fall alone, but set up a chain-reaction of disasters. A gentleman's wardrobe toppled, followed by a bookcase and hat-stand. The next half minute was filled with thuds and slidings as disturbed layers of junk resettled.

Brenton stared in disbelief. He knew there was no way out of the shop. He was now entombed.

By ten-thirty a crowd of people stood outside, his parents and PC Thorn amongst them.

Although he could not hear a word of what they said, it was obvious they were arguing with Henry Weatherby.

At ten forty-five the old man gave in. They began to empty The Fishing Shop. A line of furniture soon stretched along the pavement. More helpers arrived. Brenton sat dejectedly on a wicker chair. He could do nothing to help. There was no room for him to move anything.

It took the best part of an hour to clear the shop. At last, Brenton staggered back on to the pavement, supported by his parents. Weatherby was waiting. He muttered something about damages and sending a bill in the morning.

'Look,' said Mr Sheen. 'We've got all afternoon. There are plenty of people to help put things back and I'll pay for anything that's broken.'

This did not console Henry Weatherby.

Without waiting for his approval, several people started to lift furniture. They began with the radiogram.

'Put that back right where it was!' said a new arrival. 'Who's the owner of this lot? Ah, you! Will you take forty pounds?'

Weatherby wavered; then, nodding almost guiltily, took the money from the man.

The next sale was a double-bass that Brenton had not even noticed till then. This buyer happened to have a brother in London who reckoned he could place anything in the musical line. He took all the guitars as well as the ukulele. And that was just the beginning. The dresser that had caused all the trouble fetched a hundred-and-thirty pounds. Then word went round the Ipswich dealers and several arrived with vans. The wicker chairs – genuine Lloyd Loom, as it happened – went for thirty-five pounds a piece. Weatherby did more trade in the next few hours than he'd done in the last ten years.

Brenton and his father returned to Riverview, where the replica Vienna Regulator already hung in the hall.

They walked back to The Fishing Shop at three o'clock that afternoon. There were hardly any items left, outside or in. Weatherby's wallet was bulging.

'Forget the expenses,' he laughed as he locked up the almost empty shop. 'By the way, boy, you can have this bit!' And he gave the white dial to Brenton. 'I'll keep the bird for the flat,' he added, before disappearing up the stairs with the one-legged curlew under his arm.

Father and son walked back to Riverview once again. 'You shouldn't have done it, Brenton.'

'I know, Dad. But a real Vienna Regulator. At least I got the dial. 1873, Dad! I'm going to give it to Mum.'

'Honestly, Brenton! You shouldn't have done it. You mustn't let this clock business go to your head, you know. Marvellous hobby. But do try to keep things in proportion, Brenton. Oh well, when I was a boy of your age, I suppose I was just the same.'

British Summer Time

The thing about Uncle Bryan was he only had one car. All right – so it was a Mercedes estate with electrically-operated windows, automatic five-speed gears, power-assisted steering and quadraphonic sound. So what?

'So what?' Brenton thought as Uncle Bryan walked off to pay for his twelve gallons of petrol. Brenton's cousin Ricky sat next to him on the back seat, smiling complacently.

'What do you reckon, then?' Ricky asked him.

'Not bad,' Brenton conceded.

'That all?'

'No. It's great. Did your dad have to sell your mum's car to pay for it?'

Ricky looked at him.

'Suppose so,' he said, but quickly added, 'Dad's going to buy Mum a brand-new Mini as soon as they get back from this trip to Bruges.'

'Sounds good. But then again, what's the point in having a double garage if you don't have two cars?'

'None at all,' Ricky agreed with a shrug. Maybe Brenton's family didn't have a Merc. But their house, on the northern end of the estate, was one of the most expensive in Brayford. It wasn't called Riverview for nothing: from the master-bedroom you could see the Gippen and, beyond it, water-meadows. That view alone was worth a few thousand, Brenton's dad used to say. They also had a double garage. With two family cars they needed it.

'Excuse me,' Ricky said, leaning across Brenton and touching the button of his window so that the glass slid down with a purr. Before Brenton understood what was happening, Ricky was calling to his returning father.

'The Match-A-Cards, Dad! Did you ask for them?'

'Of course,' said Uncle Bryan, handing them through the window. 'You're welcome to them. I honestly can't be bothered with all these competitions.'

Ricky could. Before his father had settled into the driving seat, he was scratching away at the little grey oblongs with the edge of a coin.

'Five, queen, two, seven, hopeless,' he muttered. 'Four, six, king, nine, rubbish!'

'Brenton, his mind still on double garages, watched through the corner of his eye. Ricky had already set to work on a third card.

'Two, eight, jack, jack,' he said. 'Hold on, I reckon I might have something here. Dad, can you pass over the other cards?'

His father reached into the glove box and passed a handful of similar cards to Ricky.

'What are you looking for?' Brenton asked.

'What do you think?'

'Two jacks?'

'Yes, of course. I've got the jack of diamonds and the jack of clubs. What I need is another Match-A-Card with the jack of spades and the jack of hearts. Four jacks on two cards. That wins fifty pounds. Don't you even know the rules of the Delta Petrol Match-A-Card competition?'

'Course I do.'

'Well, then!'

For a moment no more was said. Ricky was examining a range of entry coupons lined out along the seat between himself and his cousin. Brenton, who knew the rules of the

115

competition inside out, was trying to look bored and yet not miss a thing. In fact he was concentrating even harder than Ricky. He had to. Though he glanced at the coupons beside him on the car seat, in his mind he was also reviewing a set of Match-A-Cards safely stored in a drawer in his bedroom.

'I've got jacks! I'm sure I have,' he told himself. 'Last week, with Dad, in Ipswich.' Which jacks they were he was not quite so sure. But one was red and the other was black. There was no doubt about that. Though he could not stop his face darkening with the desire to win, he did stop himself from speaking aloud.

He waited till the Merc had cruised down Brayford Main Street. Not till it turned into Dunlin Road did he allow himself to talk.

'If you don't want that coupon, Ricky ... If you don't want that one, I'll have it.'

'Which coupon?'

'The one with the two and the eight.'

'Oh, yeah?'

'Yes.'

'Why?'

'Because ... I mean ... well, I might as well save it.'

Ricky had already picked out the card. He was bending it between finger and thumb, almost to the point of cracking it.

'You mean the coupon with the two jacks!' he said. 'Why are you suddenly so interested?' Though Ricky was shorter than Brenton, he had the same dark hair. His eyes, too, were hard enough to match his cousin's stare.

'You've got the matching pair, haven't you? Go on, Brenton. You might as well admit it. I've got the jack of diamonds and clubs. You've got the heart and spade. Go on! Admit it. Admit it!'

The Merc glided round Plover Crescent so smoothly that they could hardly tell when Uncle Bryan switched off the engine.

'Come on, you two. Get a move on. Fiona and I have to leave in fifteen minutes if we're going to catch that ferry.'

'Well?' Ricky demanded of Brenton.

'Yes,' Brenton hissed in reply. 'If you must know I have got two jacks. Red and black. I'm sure of that. Hearts and spades, I reckon.'

Within a minute the two cousins were up in Brenton's bedroom. They placed the coupons edge to edge, neither letting go of their own. Two, eight, jack of diamonds, jack of clubs on the first; jack of hearts, seven, nine, jack of spades on the second. The numbers didn't matter: only the royal cards counted. Alone, each coupon was worth precisely nothing. Together they were worth fifty pounds cash.

Together.

That was the problem.

Saturday morning was cold and overcast, the sky a continuous grey. Neither cousin had slept well. Fifty pounds was big money. It was hard to sleep with a Match-A-Card coupon tucked under your pillow.

'Your mother and father will be in Belgium by now, Ricky. I expect they'll be having breakfast in Bruges,' said Sylvia Sheen.

Ricky began a long yawn and, not wishing to be rude, covered his mouth with a hand.

''Spect so,' he answered, as soon as his mouth was free.

After breakfast, the two boys followed the Gippen Walk all the way from Riverview down to the Ipswich Road. As soon as they'd passed the Warders' house, the road bridge came into sight. A large boy in a blue anorak was standing on it. All they could see was his top half as he leant against the parapet. Brenton recognized him.

'That's Simon Langley,' he said. 'Simon's so slow he doesn't know he's born. You'll see what I mean in a minute.'

They joined Simon on the bridge.

'What are you doing?' Brenton demanded.

'Looking at the River Gippen?' Simon suggested.

'We can see that.'

'Well, then, why ever did you ask?'

Brenton turned to his cousin and tapped his forehead with one finger. 'See what I mean?' he whispered.

Even if he had noticed, Simon wouldn't have cared. He was far more interested in the hiss and gurgle of the river. He liked the way the current rose and split against the cut-water below. Day after day old stone turning muddy water to crystal. If you stared at it long enough, you could almost believe you were standing on the prow of a boat. He liked that, too.

'Twit!' Brenton muttered.

Ricky giggled.

Brenton didn't rate Simon. Didn't rate him one bit. So it was all the more odd that something compelled him to open his mouth.

'We just won fifty pounds, me and my cousin did!'

Even now Simon did not look round, which irritated the Sheens. Slowly, he pulled a length of liquorice from his pocket. Part of a leaf and some blades of grass had stuck to it. He picked them off and turned round, chewing slowly.

'Want some?'

'No, thanks,' said Ricky.

'Didn't you hear?' Brenton insisted. 'We've won fifty

118

pounds. The Delta Petrol Match-A-Card competition. Fifty pounds! What's the matter with you? Aren't you interested?'

Simon bit off another piece of liquorice.

'So?' he asked casually.

'What d'you mean?'

'The money. Where is it?'

For a moment Ricky and Brenton felt they were almost on the same side. They pulled the coupons out of their pockets and flashed them at Simon.

'Look! Four jacks!'

'One of every suit!'

'Which one of you found 'em?'

'I did!' they both shouted.

Simon shrugged and, once more, turned to examine the river.

'Why don't you just drop 'em in the Gippen?' he said.

'Very funny!'

'It's not funny at all. You might as well face it, by themselves those cards are worth nothing.'

The twit had understood.

'Of course, you could always share the money. That way you'd both get . . .'

'You must be joking!' Ricky said.

'That's right!' snapped Brenton with family pride. 'We're not like you, Simon. Ricky and me aren't the type to give in. With us Sheens, it's all or nothing.'

'In that case, there's only one thing for it. You'll have to call a Bus Stop, Brenton.'

'What's a bus stop?' demanded Ricky, a stranger to village ways.

Neither Simon nor Brenton answered him.

'Can you fix it for this afternoon?' Brenton asked.

'Reckon so.'

'Normal arrangements?'

Simon nodded. The two cousins walked off, Ricky none the wiser.

'What on earth's a bus stop?' he asked again.

'A Bus Stop is just what it says, Ricky.'

'But you go to a bus stop to catch a bus.'

'Not if you live in Brayford.'

The bus service between Brayford and Ipswich was a dead loss. Once upon a time things had been reasonable, with buses at twenty-seven minutes past each hour. Then the bus company had cut its service by half. 'That's progress for you!' the locals complained. And as if to punish them for it, the company decided that no sane person could possibly want to go into Ipswich after three twenty-seven. It was now little more than a skeleton service. All of which explains why the bus shelter opposite the chestnut trees on the Lower Green had fallen into disuse. Like all places that grown-ups abandon, it immediately held an irresistible attraction for children.

So they had started meetings – or Bus Stops, as they called them. These were lively affairs. The intention was to hold courts, sort out plans and keep stock of village matters with an eye to the advantage of children. None of which Brenton had explained to his cousin by the time they reached the bus shelter that Saturday afternoon.

'I still haven't got a clue what's happening!'

'You'll soon see.'

'We don't go to bus stops in Leicester,' Ricky said. 'Sometimes a bunch of us go to a football match or a film. But why go to bus stops?'

'It must be dull living in Leicester,' Brenton commented. He looked at his cousin as if to say, 'You poor little city kid!'

When they entered the shelter of metal and glass, clutching their Match-A-Cards, they found it full of other children.

'Good, the Committee's here,' Brenton explained. 'As you're a stranger, I'll introduce you. This is Melvyn Maddock. You call him Mr President. He acts as a leader or judge.'

Melvyn – as burly and vigorous as his father, the butcher – called out a greeting.

'And then there's Simon Langley who you've already met on the bridge. Simon may look stupid – he probably is. But remember, he called this Bus Stop for us. So you mind your manners.'

Brenton then introduced the rest of the bunch. Sally Warder, the fastest runner in Brayford. Her friend, Rachel Conners (who listened but seldom spoke). Dean Fulcher –

121

so violent that when he was away on holiday he'd been banned from Bus Stops by a unanimous vote but when he came back still joined in because nobody dared to tell him. Finally there was a girl who looked about thirteen. She turned out to be Alabama Candy. Her father was an American serviceman. She had only lived in Brayford for a month or two; but at five foot eleven she was taller than most adults and had become a legend in her own time.

'And who's that?' asked Ricky, pointing outside through the side window to a boy with a round face and glasses.

'That's Gregory Stuart. We just call him Greg. He knows the bus times inside out. You have to check with him before you call a Bus Stop: Greg is also the brainiest kid in Brayford.'

'Not much competition!' Ricky sniggered.

'Shut up,' his cousin ordered. 'Shut up and listen.'

Gregory was calling to them.

'The next bus is the three twenty-seven,' he explained. 'That gives you thirty-two minutes, so you better get started.'

It didn't take long to get to the problem.

Exhibit A – two, eight, jack, jack.

Exhibit B – jack, seven, nine, jack.

Somebody managed to wedge the cards into the window frame on the left. Sitting on the bench that ran along the back of the shelter, the Bus Stop members could stare at the cards and dream of the fifty pounds. Or, if they chose, they could look past the chestnut-trees to the footbridge over the River Gippen and, beyond that, to the slope of the Upper Green.

Still outside, Gregory stepped closer to the window. He thought they were trying to pass some message to him.

Dean Fulcher waved him away. No one else paid much attention.

Then Melvyn Maddock stood up solemnly, blocking out much of the landscape. He summoned Ricky and Brenton to stand by his side. After they had sworn a few oaths, Melvyn returned to the centre of the bench. There followed four or five minutes of questioning.

'Anything to add?' Melvyn asked them.

'No.'

'No.'

'And you're still determined not to share the money?'

'Yes.'

'Yes.'

'And you won't toss a coin or pick straws?'

'No.'

'No.'

'Right, then. We have a full shelter today. So, as Mr President, I invite those present to offer their suggestions.'

123

Nobody spoke. They all admired Melvyn for the way he handled things. (His father sat on Brayford Parish Council and, as he often told Mrs Maddock about meetings, Melvyn had been able to pick up some useful jargon.)

After the silence Melvyn moved that a contest was the only solution.

The Bus Stop, calm and attentive till now, suddenly went wild. Dean Fulcher was calling for a fist fight: the first to draw blood would be the winner. It was simple. Why waste time? He was so excited by the idea of blood that he jumped up, swinging a hand into Alabama Candy's rib.

'Cool it!' she warned. 'Cool it, buddy!'

He snarled at her but held back his temper as she stood up, towering over him.

'Order! Order!' Melvyn commanded. 'Sally. Where are you going?'

She explained that she had to nip out to see her brother. He stood crying on the far side of the road. She thought he must have stung himself on some nettles or something.

'Don't you have any ideas before you go?'

Anxious that her brother should not cross the road alone, Sally spoke in a hurry.

'A race,' she said. 'Just hold a running race.'

'Great idea!' Candy agreed.

'But I'll lose!' Ricky complained. 'I can tell you that now. Brenton's a year older than me. I wouldn't stand a chance!'

Simon Langley, who'd been last in every race he'd ever entered, agreed this was quite unfair. They had to think up something that gave both cousins a chance.

'Water biscuits,' he suggested.

'That's disgusting,' Rachel Conners complained.

'Why?' asked Ricky. 'What d'you have to do?'

'Don't you know? They give you a pile of water biscuits – the dry ones people eat with cheese. Whoever eats the most before their jaws gunge up is the winner.'

'Sounds all right to me,' said Ricky.

'Brenton, do you accept?'

'No, I don't, Mr President. Don't you remember when John Frazer and Gareth Thomas tried it and they both got stuck on the sixth biscuit and Gareth ended up being sick? I've still got some pride left! Anyway, why should I lose fifty pounds just because my cousin can stuff himself better?'

'I can see his point of view,' Melvyn ruled. 'In the end biscuit-stuffing comes down to a question of spit.'

Dean leapt up. It was hard to tell whether his face was twisted by a smile or a snarl.

'Great idea!' he leered. 'Let's cut the cackle and hold a spitting contest. Best distance. Three gobs each.'

The president and members just ignored him.

Suddenly Gregory walked along the front of the shelter and peered in, as if he badly wanted to tell them something.

'I've got it,' said Melvyn, before Gregory could speak. 'Brain power. We'll get Greg to think up one of his teasers. He'll set the problem and the first one to solve it . . .'

This was one of Melvyn's rare slips. Already the Committee groaned. They had tried this on two boys before to sort out a violent row over a pound coin. After an hour both boys had given up.

'Here's one,' Gregory announced proudly. It was too late. They couldn't stop him.

'Two men catch a train to visit their aunts in a town one hundred miles away. The train leaves at . . .'

'That's enough, Greg!'

'. . . at eight o'clock precisely. It travels at forty miles an hour for the first twenty miles, fifty miles an hour for the next twenty miles and ...'

'We got you!' said Candy. 'Sixty miles an hour for the next twenty miles.'

'No, no. After forty miles the first man gets off at a station. He goes to the buffet and asks for a cheese sandwich and three pickled onions.'

'For heaven's sake, Greg!'

'That's fine. We've heard enough.'

'Unfortunately, there are only two pickled onions left in the jar. So he leaves the buffet and waits for the next train, which was due an hour later than the one he caught but was delayed by thirty minutes.'

Melvyn ordered him officially to shut up and told him, officially, that he was a pain.

'Please yourselves,' Gregory said. He didn't sound hurt. He just smiled and went back to his spot on the pavement. But before the members could return to their business, Gregory was tapping on the window. He was pointing to the back of the Match-A-Cards.

'I just wanted to say ...'

'Thank you, Greg, You can save your brain-teaser for another occasion.'

'Yes, but ...'

'No buts. We've got other things to worry about.'

Gregory was staring at the back of the cards. He was re-reading the competition rules. He mouthed the words. Nobody listened. Nobody even watched him.

Suddenly, Mrs Trinder appeared. She was about fifty yards away, on the corner of Main Street and the Ipswich road. Since her husband had died, she always walked very slowly. Gregory didn't look at his watch. There was no point – it was broken. Not that he minded. There were plenty of ways to tell the time. Mrs Trinder, for instance.

It would be about three-fifteen. She never missed the three twenty-seven.

He was about to walk back into the shelter to tell the Bus Stop president that time was up when Alabama Candy came striding out, followed by Simon and Melvyn.

'I've been trying to tell you. The rules state quite clearly . . .'

'Don't you try to tell me the rules!' Melvyn warned. 'After all, I haven't been elected president three times in a row for nothing!'

'Yes, but time has run out!'

'We know that. But it doesn't matter, Greg. We've just found a solution.'

By the time Mrs Trinder climbed on to the bus, the members were on their way home.

Well before midnight everything was set up according to Bus Stop instructions. It was not possible for officials to be with them, but the Sheen cousins could be trusted. They had placed the two chairs about five feet apart. The Delta Petrol Match-A-Card coupons were laid out on the carpet, exactly halfway between them. No books were allowed. No form of entertainment. It was just a question of sitting it out. Melvyn Maddock had explained it all twice over. The first person to nod off lost his card and, of course, the cash.

They waited another minute. Then, as the new hall clock chimed delicately from below, the boys took up their positions.

A question of endurance. A question of time.

By twelve-thirty both of them felt an ache in the small of their backs. Neither admitted it. Neither spoke. For speaking was also against Bus Stop regulations.

It was odd, too, how their bottoms ached. Bottoms

were meant to be good for sitting on, but they weren't as efficient as all that – not by a quarter to one.

Ricky's main tactic was to think of things he liked. Dad's new two-litre Merc, for instance. His parents had been due to catch the return ferry from Zeebrugge at eleven o'clock that evening. Now the Merc would be down on the car deck. Mum and Dad would be sleeping in their cabin. By seven-thirty the next morning they'd arrive in Brayford. Maybe he'd be fifty pounds richer by then.

Suddenly Ricky jolted. He stared at his cousin. Brenton's head had sunk a little lower. Already! Maybe this was it. As far as he could tell, Brenton's eyelids were closed. Ricky eased his bottom off the chair. It creaked and, immediately, Brenton thrust up his head. He rubbed the muscles in the back of his neck. The clock downstairs gave out a single, distant chime. 'Not this time,' Ricky thought. 'Not now. But it won't be long.' He realized that he was shaking. Even when he felt calm again, he was shaking. The room, with the central heating no longer on, was bitterly cold.

Brenton had noticed it too. The cold was almost worse than the ache in his neck. Yet there were advantages in aches and pains. If they could ward off sleep, they were worth fifty pounds. And as if the cold were not enough, Brenton tried the opposite technique to Ricky: he conjured up a sequence of nasty thoughts ...

'If I nod off,' he kept telling himself, 'Ricky will go home laughing. Of course the story will be all round Leicester in no time. Leicester! What am I thinking of? Never mind Leicester. What about Brayford? If I don't have fifty pounds to wave at people, I'm going to be laughed out of existence. Louts like Dean Fulcher, giggling their heads off. Simon Langley saying, "You should have shared it, shouldn't you!" Silly old woman! I can hear him now.

128

And Gregory. Even Gregory . . .' Suddenly he remembered the strange round face; the smile; the glasses that kept slipping off the bridge of his nose. How soft Gregory was! And yet, how dangerous. And before he knew it, Brenton had pictured a crazy scene in a railway buffet. A couple of pickled onions sat in a jar on the counter. A man rushed in through the door, clutching a railway ticket. Forty miles an hour for the first twenty miles, fifty miles an hour for the next twenty miles, sixty miles an hour . . . only two pickled onions. Oh, no! It was all so stupid. It was making him sleepy just to think of it. Greg! Mad-brained Greg. How could anybody make a hobby out of timetables?

Brenton was startled by a moan from Ricky. This was it! He was keeling over. If he fell off the chair, he lost automatically. He lost if he fell asleep. 'Oh . . .' he moaned again. His head slumped downward . . .

Fifty quid! Ricky had nodded off. Fifty quid! Jack, jack, jack, jack. Brenton looked at the cards on the carpet: his mind turned them into bank notes. But when he looked up again, Ricky was smiling. He fixed Brenton with a nauseating stare and slowly shook his head.

Pretending, was he? So that was it! Well, two could play at that game. It was against all Bus Stop regulations. All right. He could play dirty as well. 'You just wait, Ricky Sheen! You just wait.'

Both cousins were shivering with cold now. They had to keep their bottoms on the chairs. All they could do was rotate their shoulders, clench and unclench their hands. Then three chimes sounded from the hall.

Five minutes later, Brenton did it deliberately. He let his head tilt sideways, chin resting on his collar-bone. And it worked. A minute later he heard Ricky move. He had fallen for it!

'Go on, then,' he thought. 'Go and pick it up.'

129

Ricky did. Brenton could not see him or hear him any more. But he sensed his greedy fingers clasping at the cards, snatching them up from the carpet. And the next moment, Ricky had climbed into bed, the cards no doubt in his hand.

'Fine. Enjoy yourself,' Brenton mused. 'Go to sleep now, Baby Bunting.'

Three-ten. Stealthily Brenton rose from his chair. His cousin was out for the count. It was not difficult to lift the corner of his blanket, nor to prise the two coupons from his grip. Not completely honest, it was true. But then again, Ricky had asked for trouble. Hadn't he pretended to sleep a little earlier? That smile! That taunt! He had asked for it.

By three-twenty both cousins slept like lambs. Outside, snow fell, silent and magical. The night was dark and soundless. Seventy miles out at sea, snow also fell on the deck of a ferry as it bore the Merc and her sleeping owners across the dark waters towards Felixstowe.

And it seemed that hardly a moment had passed before Uncle Bryan and Aunt Fiona stepped into the room. Before he had even said hello, Ricky snatched up his pillow and searched the bedclothes frantically.

'Brenton! You sneak! You little reptile! You can't!'

Brenton rolled over and yawned complacently. The fact was, he had.

At breakfast neither cousin spoke. Brenton, despite his victory, was yawning like a hippo. Ricky Sheen refused all food and, as he opened his parents' present of Belgian chocolates, hardly managed a thank-you.

He glanced at his watch. Six forty-five.

'Six forty-five!' he gasped. 'Surely that's wrong. You weren't due till seven-thirty. Surely that's wrong, Dad.

That's wrong!'

'No, it isn't,' laughed Bryan Sheen. 'I'm afraid you lost a bit of sleep last night. Don't you realize it's March 27th. The clocks went forward an hour last night. Don't you realize – we're in British Summer Time. All the same, you can mind your manners, Ricky. An hour in bed's nothing to worry about. Boys like you should be able to lose a little sleep without all this fussing and whining!'

A thin layer of snow had settled on the lawn and also on the roof of the bus shelter where Gregory sat alone.

He wasn't thinking of trains and pickled onions but of four jacks on two Match-A-Cards.

More precisely, he remembered the rules. Not Bus Stop regulations, as set out by the president – but the rules of the Delta Petrol Match-A-Card Game. *Competition ends on March 26th.* He had seen the date through the side window yesterday. No doubt about it. But would they listen?

He had tried to tell them. He really had.

It was all just a question of time.

Dead Man's Boots

It was April 3rd. Easter Day. The Wright family entered
the church, knelt for a few moments (bottoms squashed
against the pew), sat up again and waited for the service
to begin.

'There's Mrs Trinder,' said Mr Wright. 'Marvellous,
really, how she manage to keep that post office going all
on her own. Let's see now,' he calculated. 'November,
December, January, February, March. That's near enough
six month her husband been dead.'

The twins, Jenny and Jodie, looked at each other. *Dead.
Dead.* A shadow crossed their faces at exactly the same
moment. They had almost forgotten till now. Not that
they had known old Trinder that well. Just a man from the
village really. In the daytime they used to see him behind
the post-office counter. On warm evenings he would sit
outside the Crown and Anchor – always on the same
bench, just inside the porch. Since they were three or four
the twins had watched him from their bedroom window.
Through every summer he seemed to have sat there, sucking his pipe and staring at passers-by. Enormous and
gentle. Never talkative, but always kindly. Then one
autumn – last autumn – the nights drew in early and they
guessed he drank his beer and sucked his pipe indoors.

They were wrong.

And oddly, when he died and Mum came into the kitchen
and said, 'There's something sad happen and I reckon you
two ought to know,' the twins had felt nothing. They were

sorry. But feeling sorry wasn't feeling sorrow.

Only now, as they caught sight of Mrs Trinder in the church, did they feel a real twinge.

'That's an awful shame. We liked him,' Jenny said.

The vicar appeared at the front of the nave and the service began.

'Yip, we really liked him,' Jodie agreed in a whisper.

'Sh! You two! Just stop talking!' their father ordered.

'How long ago did Dad say that happen?'

'That make six month, according to Dad,' Jenny answered. 'November, December, January . . .'

'I'm telling you, if you don't stop it, I'll take the pair of you out of the church in front of everyone.'

This didn't seem very fair to the twins, since it was really their dad who had started the conversation. But they quietened down. It wasn't too bad, once they got to the singing.

As soon as the service was over, they were up on their feet.

'You sit down again!' Mrs Wright told them. 'What's got into you both? You trying to beat the vicar out of the church or something?'

At last the other people in their pew stood up. Dad, who was a tall man, knocked a prayer mat off its hook, bent down, fumbled for it and straightened up again. As he moved into the aisle, his round wife behind him, he came face to face with old Trinder's widow. She smiled at him, then mouthed a soundless 'hello'. Slowly she raised a hand and gestured to Mr Wright to move past with his family. By the time they had done so, the smile on her face had gone.

Outside, the Reverend Morley was shaking hands with the congregation, one by one.

'Lovely to see you, Mrs Parks. How's the little grandson? Hello! Here are the twins. Have you had your Easter eggs yet? Well, don't eat too much chocolate! Nice to see you in church, Mr Wright ... Ah, Mrs Trinder! There you are! Happy Easter! How are things?'

He took both her hands gently in his own – almost as if to warm them.

'Funny, them little benches!' Jodie said. For the twins, thinking of home and their chocolate, already stood beneath the roof of the lychgate. They sat down, one on each side of the little stone building.

'Why do grown-ups always dawdle so much?' Jenny complained.

Jodie shrugged. The benches they sat on, and the little stone building itself, reminded her of the porch outside the Crown and Anchor.

'They'll be stood there all morning if we don't jostle 'em along,' Jenny continued. 'Just look at 'em jawing. Come

on, Jodie. Come on.'

As they took the path back towards the church, Easter bells suddenly pealed from the tower.

There was no white surplice. The vicar had gone. That wasn't the problem. Their mother and father and Mrs Trinder still talked on without him.

'Better wait here,' Jenny advised. It looked like grown-up conversation.

And yet – though their voices were drowned by the waves of sound from the bell tower – none of the grown-ups seemed really sad. Suddenly a high tinkle of laughter burst from Mrs Trinder. It startled the twins. They took a step closer; but already the laughter was over.

'Reckon they are pretty big,' said the widow, her voice dry and thin again. She was staring down at their father's feet. 'You got to admit to that, Mr Wright. So go on, you might as well have 'em.'

'Well, if you think your Trevor wouldn't have minded . . .' Mr Wright began.

'Blooming carthorse, you are, Eric!' their mother interrupted. 'They should have an enclosure for men like you, down at the Suffolk Show!'

The twins smiled. It was true their dad had big feet. Woppers! Like old Trinder, he was a big man – nearly six foot two.

At last the Wright family set off. Arm in arm they walked in a line that only just fitted on the path. They had to break into twos to pass through the lychgate. Jodie wrapped her arm round her mum; Jenny reached up to take her dad's hand.

Mrs Trinder waited behind in the graveyard. Suddenly she called after them. 'I'll drop 'em round for you this afternoon.'

Mr Wright said that'd do fine.

135

By the time Sunday dinner was over, he seemed to have forgotten all about the boots.

'What we all need is a walk,' he declared. 'The fresh air will do us good.'

'I don't need fresh air like he do 'cos I never drunk too much beer with my dinner!' whispered Jenny.

'And I don't need fresh air like he do,' added Jodie. ''cos I never ate eight potatoes!'

Mr Wright stood at the kitchen sink, scrubbing away at a saucepan. In his hands it looked like a toy. Even the sink seemed to shrink to half its size when Dad did the washing-up. It reminded the twins of their headteacher, Mr Gibson. He used to crawl into the Wendy House to be friendly with the Infants. They were mostly frightened he would bust their plastic cooker. One day he did his back in and, after that, he stayed in the grown-up world where he belonged.

'You two hurry up and get yourselves ready,' Mr Wright said.

'Can't we stay indoors?'

'And play in our bedroom?'

'No, you can't. You're too young to stay in the house by yourselves. Your mum would have a fit.'

'No, she wouldn't,' Jenny replied. 'You have a look in the living room, Dad.'

He did. He found his wife with her feet up on the settee. A half-finished cup of tea stood on a low table near her. On the floor between the table and the settee lay a crumpled newspaper. Mrs Wright smiled in her sleep. He did not have the heart to wake her.

'Well, I'm going to the Top Green to look at the daffodils,' he whispered. 'If you want to stay, you can do. But don't you go thumping about the house or hollering your heads off. And, another thing – don't you open the door. Not to anyone.'

As soon as they were alone, they took out their boxes. They had been saving them up for some time. They also fetched out felt-tip pens and began to decorate the sides and the lids with eggs that were far too round. Jodie then drew a tiny creature with triangular wings.

'That a chick or an angel?' asked Jenny.

Jodie, no longer certain herself, began to colour it in.

'I never saw pink chicks before!' said Jenny.

'Well, then, that's an angel.'

'I never saw angels popping out of eggs!'

Jodie just shrugged her shoulders.

'And anyway,' Jenny added, 'angels isn't Easter. Angels is Christmas time.'

Twenty minutes later, the boxes were almost ready. They lined the insides with Kleenex, split open the eggs that their parents had given them, took out the chocolates that lay inside and placed five or six of them in each of their boxes.

They were just writing *Happy Easter Mum and Dad* when the doorbell rang.

'Don't you open that!' said Jenny.

She wasn't joking.

'And don't you go too near that window, neither.'

The bell rang a second time. They listened for the sound of movement below; but it did not come and they knew that their mother slept on. Maybe she was still smiling. From where they waited, they could not see the pavement below. All they could safely see was the empty road and, beyond that, the empty porch of the Crown and Anchor.

The caller rang once again, then knocked on the door timidly. By now each twin had moved back to her bed. They sat on the covers, their feet tucked under their bottoms.

Neither spoke.

Two minutes later Jenny moved to the window. She opened it and cautiously peered down.

'Boots!' she said.

'What?'

'Reckon that was Mrs Trinder. She brought them boots round for Dad.'

Both leant out properly now and saw the enormous Wellingtons on the doorstep by the empty milk bottles. From above they looked horribly sad – like black and empty caverns.

'We can't just leave 'em sitting outside,' said Jenny. 'Reckon we best fetch 'em in.'

A moment later they were by the front door.

'They're dead ... They're dead man's boots!' gasped Jodie.

'Don't be daft!'

'They are. I'm not touching 'em!'

As they stared at them through the open door, the boots looked even more threatening.

'You can pick 'em up,' Jodie whispered. 'Go on! You're the oldest!'

'Only by nine minutes.'

'You scared as well, then?'

Irritated by this, the older twin stepped out to take them, turned and strode in again. The Wellingtons, carried one in each hand, bumped and thumped her ankles, almost touching the ground.

'Out the way!' she ordered, hurrying down the corridor as if to be rid of the Wellingtons as fast as possible.

She didn't believe in ghosts, but there was no point in encouraging them.

'Move out the way!' she repeated. 'Shut the door, for heaven's sake – but don't slam it, or you'll wake Mum up.'

Jodie did as she was told, then followed her twin to the back of the house to see her put the boots down in the middle of the kitchen.

'What do we do now, Jenny! We can't just leave 'em there.'

'You got any ideas for a change?'

'Nope.'

For the next minute they stared at the boots. It made them feel small just to look at them.

'What was that ... What was that you called 'em, Jodie?'

'Dead man's boots, 'cos that's what they are. Do you reckon Dad'll really put 'em on?'

'Maybe,' Jenny answered. Then her voice cracked. 'Dead man's boots? No! He can't! We have to stop him!'

'We have to stop him,' Jodie agreed. 'But how?'

'We could prong 'em.'

'What are you talking about, Jenny?'

'Prong 'em – so Dad have to throw 'em away! We could prong 'em with a garden fork.'

'But the shed's locked up. So there's no chance of that.'

'Well then, we better skewer 'em,' Jenny suggested.

'You mean with kebab sticks.'

'Yip. Why not? We could skewer 'em now, while Mum's still asleep.'

'But Dad'll see we done it, as soon as he come in.'

'Not if we just kebab 'em a bit.'

'Then he wouldn't see the holes at all, Jenny. And by the time he realize, that would be too late – the dead man's boots would be on his feet.'

'You got any ideas?' Jenny asked.

'Bury 'em,' said Jodie.

'What with?'

'Earth.'

'Yip. But what'll we dig it with?'

'A spade, Jenny. A spade.'

'No chance.'

'Why not?'

'That's also locked in the shed.'

'Well, we're going to have to think of something.'

Silence.

'Shame we can't get them boots to shrink!' Jenny mused. She knew it was a ridiculous thing to say, but she was glad to hear her sister giggling. 'Come to that,' she added, 'that's a shame Dad's feet aren't even bigger. Either way, them blessed boots wouldn't fit!'

Jodie giggled again.

'Maybe we could run the tops through Mum's sewing-machine,' she suggested.

'Too noisy,' said Jenny, 'but I'll tell you what – we could always fill 'em up with concrete!'

'I know. I got it!' Jodie exclaimed. 'We could melt 'em in the oven. Two black puddles!'

'Best idea yet. Imagine Dad's face, Jodie! *Tea's ready, Dad . . . Oh no! Not rubber omelettes again!*'

'You're mad, Jenny!'

'That was your idea.'

Suddenly they heard another voice. They froze. It was Dad on the doorstep.

'Is somebody going to open this door or not?' he called.

The boots still stood on the kitchen tiles. Once again Jenny grabbed them.

'What are you doing?'

'Hiding 'em up.'

'Up where?'

'Upstairs. Come on!'

They flew up, three steps at a time, and cornered sharply into their parents' bedroom. Jenny pulled back the doors of the built-in cupboard, plonked the boots in amongst the shoes, rearranged the coats and dresses, slid the door back and walked with Jodie down to the hall again.

Their father had just put some daffodils down on a chair. Mrs Wright, although she had opened the door to her husband, was still only half-awake as he took off his coat.

'That's wrong to pick wild flowers,' Jenny panted.

'Not if you pick 'em for Mrs Trinder,' he said. 'Nothing wrong in that. Anyway, what have you been up to, Little Miss Perfect?'

'Nothing.'

'Nothing very much at all,' Jodie added.

'Let's see if you can help me with tea,' said Dad. 'Mrs Trinder should be here in a minute or two. She got some old boots for me.'

Neither twin spoke.

He went to the kitchen and filled the kettle. Mum said she was going to tidy herself up a bit.

'Posh cups for Easter Day!' Dad announced. He lifted them down from the dresser – thimble-sized in his enormous hands.

Jenny, setting out knives and sideplates, glanced helplessly at her sister.

'We should have chucked 'em over a hedge,' she whispered. 'Got rid of 'em – not stood there joking!'

Which is when Mrs Wright screamed.

It ripped the air. Four, five seconds. A long, high, slicing sound.

'Lord above! She gone and electrified herself!' Dad shouted.

They saw their mother tumbling down the stairs.

'What on earth . . .'

'A man! Oh, Eric! A man in the cupboard!'

141

'Right!' said the father. 'All of you – into the kitchen! I'll get him. Leave it to me!'

'Eric! Be careful! He could be armed.'

But it was too late for warnings. Mr Wright had reached the landing.

'You hear me!' he roared. 'You are going to come out of that room or – I warn you – I'm coming in!'

Downstairs nobody spoke. All three were trembling.

'I said, you come out! You come out right now, if you're any kind of a man!'

A door creaked.

Jenny gasped. Jodie began to cry. Both twins shut their eyes and buried their faces against the quivering body of their mother. Then came the footsteps. Silence. Footsteps again. They forced themselves to look upward. And there he stood, as large as life ...

It was Dad, standing on the landing. His head shook in anger. An enormous boot dangled from each of his massive hands.

At seven o'clock that evening, the twins went up to their bedroom. Neither of them even tried to sleep. Cars turned into the small car park by the side of the Crown and Anchor. Car doors slammed, greetings were called and, before long, choruses of laughter spilt out of the crowded pub.

'Well, that's a lovely way to end Easter Day!' their mother had grumbled. 'First you scare the living daylights out of me, then you go into a two-hour sulk. No wonder me and your father get riled!'

'Sorry, Mum.'

'Sorry, Mum.'

'Sometime "sorry" don't do. You finish your meat and jacket potatoes and then you get to bed.'

It didn't seem fair. It never did. If anybody was sulking, it was their dad. As they'd gone upstairs, he'd left for the pub. Said he'd be back in half an hour, with some cider and crisps for Mum.

An hour later he still wasn't back. They tried to catch his voice in the chorus. Maybe he sat at a table alone. Could be he was still sulking.

It was just after nine that he came back in. They could tell that his mood had changed.

'Sally! Sally! I brought back your crisps. I also brought back some visitors!'

'Sh! You'll wake the twins!'

'Here's your cider! And here's Mrs Trinder! Tom – you get that beer open!'

Both twins sat up in their beds.

'Sorry. I'm forgetting my manners, dear! This is ... well, you know Mrs Trinder ...' (he seemed to find this incredibly funny) '... and this is her son, Tom. Tom's drove over from Stowmarket to cheer his mum up a bit!'

To the twins the noise of the pub seemed at last to have dropped. Or rather, a good part of it seemed to have slipped across the street and into their living room.

'Oh – and thank you for them boots,' Mr Wright added.

'Do they fit?' asked Mrs Trinder.

'Perfectly ... Well, to tell you the truth, I haven't yet tried 'em on. Now, listen, Mrs Trinder – I must tell you a little story about your Trevor's boots! Listen. You're going to like this! You see, when you called round, Sally was asleep and I was picking the daffodils. Hold on! Sally! We forgot! Quick! Get the daffodils!'

Amongst the popping of cans and the clinking of glasses, Dad told the whole story.

'... and I thought the old girl had gone and electrified herself. By golly, did she holler!'

143

'And then Eric stood outside the bedroom,' Mrs Wright added, roaring with laughter. "You come out now!" he starts shouting "You come out right now, if you're any sort of a man!"'

More laughing.

'Go on, Mrs Trinder. One more little glass of sherry won't do you any harm!'

'Well, just a small one. And thank you – thank you for the daffodils.'

She laughed too. The same fluttering laugh that they had heard outside the church. But this time it did not stop. She laughed again and again.

Jenny suddenly rolled out of bed. She leant over her twin sister and whispered into her ear.

'You wouldn't!' Jodie whispered back. 'That's lying, and lying's wrong!'

'So's picking wild daffodils, but that's what he done!'

The four grown-ups in the living room were slowly recovering. Mrs Wright was passing round a box of Kleenex. They now blew their noses, mopped their brows and wiped their eyes. Mrs Trinder was leaning against Tom. She had got a stitch from laughing.

Mr Wright suddenly set off again with a splutter of giggles. He held some of it back, but little snorts escaped through his nose. 'If you're any sort of man . . .' he blurted out.

'Oh, stop it, Eric!' Mrs Wright pleaded. 'That really crack me up!'

He did stop this time.

The door swung open. The twins, in yellow pyjamas, edged into the room. Each carried a giant Wellington. Neither of them smiled.

'We come to say sorry,' Jenny said.

'Sorry,' Jodie added.

Mrs Wright turned towards them, knocking an empty beer can off the coffee table.

'That's all right, children,' she said. 'We know you never meant anything by it. Just didn't think. That's all. You just didn't think.'

Jenny looked at her.

'We did, Mum. We did think. It was meant to be a surprise.'

'By heck! That come as a bit more than a surprise!' Mr Wright exclaimed. 'Another surprise like that and you'll finish your mother off!'

'No, we never meant to scare no one! We done presents, see.'

All four adults stared at Jenny and then at Jodie. Meekly they stepped forward. Jenny placed her Wellington boot in front of Mr Wright; Jodie offered hers to her mother.

'What do you mean?' Mrs Wright asked. 'Them boots come from Mrs Trinder.'

'Just look inside, Mum,' Jenny explained. 'You have to tip 'em over.'

'Or else,' Jodie added, 'you could just stick your hand in.'

The parents hesitated. They then picked the boots up and slowly tilted them.

A small, decorated box slid out of each Wellington. Which box was first to land on the carpet it was difficult to say. Nobody noticed anyway. It was a matter of seconds.

'Oh, the little angels!' Mrs Trinder sighed.

Both parents kissed each twin. Mr Wright went to fetch some Coke and two more glasses from the kitchen.

An hour later they went upstairs again. The last sound the twins heard before they slept was Mrs Trinder laughing as Tom walked her home.

Nuts in May

'Reckon that could be one. Reckon that could!' Jodie suggested after breakfast on Friday morning.

She was sitting on the edge of her twin bed, her pyjama top rolled up just above the belly button, the index finger of her right hand pressed against her belly.

'Reckon that's a spot all right,' she insisted.

Jenny – whose face, chest, back, arms and thighs glowed with a thousand pin-points – Jenny said, 'Yip, that is. But one spot don't mean the measles. One spot's nothing.'

'Could be the start.'

'Not unless you feel all flushed ... Do you feel all flushed, Jodie?'

'Nope.'

'Got a throb in your head?'

'Nope.'

'Git dizzy when you stand up?'

Jodie stood up and waited a few seconds ...

'Nope.'

'Thirst? You parched with thirst, then?'

'Nope.'

'Aches in your joints – you got them?'

'Yip. They do ache a bit.'

'Ah! But that have to ache a lot. Do they? Do they ache a lot?'

'Nope.'

'Well, then, you never got 'em, and that's that.'

Jenny had spoken with some pride. *She* should know.

146

Oh yes! *She* knew the difference between the measles and one spot. At first light that very morning, she had woken up aching from head to foot and as parched as a desert. It was lovely, being ill – once you got used to it. No school. Boiled egg and toasted fingers in bed, a pile of comics, a new colouring book.

'Do I git egg and toasted fingers too?' Jodie had asked irritably.

'You most likely will,' her mother said.

Jodie got an egg for breakfast and was let off going to school.

What she didn't get was the measles.

That afternoon Jenny was moved to her parents' own bedroom. Mrs Wright insisted that Jodie share the double bed with her sister.

'If Jenny have it, then you better have it too,' she explained. 'That's best to catch the measles while you're still nice and young.'

But, as things turned out, it was not like sleeping in the same bed – more like staying awake in the same bed. Especially the first night. Jenny said that Dad was so heavy he'd turned his side of the mattress into a crater. Jodie swore that Mum's side was worse. Maybe Dad's crater was deep, but she'd lay a bet any day, Mum's was a deal wider.

Meanwhile their parents were tossing and turning – each in their twin bed. Unused to the front room that looked out on to Brayford Main Street, they were woken by every passing motorbike or car. Although Mr Wright lay with his head against the headboard, his feet stuck out half a metre beyond the blankets. Mrs Wright, on the other hand, rolled over perilously every minute. Instead of coming to rest against the solid bulk of her husband, she would awake to find the whole bed listing badly and her body overflowing into the night.

'I like a bed that give room to manoeuvre!' Mr Wright grumbled on the Saturday morning. 'If I can't manoeuvre, I can't sleep. It's as simple as that!'

Sunday morning he said it again. Mrs Wright was growing tired of hearing it.

'Rome weren't built in a day,' she pointed out.

Mr Wright said he didn't see how Rome came into it.

'You know what I mean – the twins, Eric. We can't expect Jodie to catch measles just like that. We have to give it a day or two. Jenny were always the forward one. You know that!'

It was true. First Jenny; then Jodie. That was the way of it. Jenny had even been born first – just nine minutes in the lead. 'I'm the oldest!' she would say, whether people asked her or not.

But what did nine minutes matter?

Nothing, except that Jenny was the first to say 'Mumma!', the first to crawl and then walk. Nothing, except that she was out of nappies slightly before her sister. Even now she tended to speak out more readily, to raise her hand in class more eagerly, to reach out for door handles more swiftly. 'You're the oldest? Ah, well you'll be first!' giggled teachers and doctors and Father Christmases. It didn't matter much. Jodie didn't mind. She was used to it. She'd be the last to complain.

'Jenny first; then Jodie,' Mrs Wright stated.

But by the Monday morning – May Day as it happened – she didn't sound so sure.

Nobody could understand this break in the pattern. Jenny had woken up last Friday dizzy and hot and spotty. Nine minutes later Jodie had nothing. No queer spells, no parched throat. Three whole days and nights later and . . .

'I told you one spot never meant the measles,' the elder

148

twin reminded her.

Jodie sat up in her parents' double bed and examined her belly button.

'Reckon you're right,' she told her sister.

Even the spot had now gone.

'We could do Scrabble,' Jenny said, late on Monday after-noon. Jodie, who had spent much of the day watching her sister sleep, said, 'Yip, we could do Scrabble,' and went to fetch the box from their own bedroom.

'Did I have lunch?' Jenny asked sleepily.

'Yip. Clear soup and toasted fingers.'

'What did you have, Jodie?'

'Cold chicken, tomatoes, lettuce, jacket potatoes and lemon meringue pie.'

'Any chicken left?'

'Nope.'

'Where's Mum and Dad?'

'Gardening. I saw 'em go out.'

'Well, then, Jodie, do us a favour! Nip downstairs to the kitchen.'

'What for?'

'How would I know? Whatever you can find. Go on, Jodie. Try the fridge. Go on. You nip down and fetch me something nice. Go on – before we do Scrabble.'

While Jodie raided the kitchen, her sister set up the game on the covers of the double bed. Even when she was quite well, she preferred to play Scrabble upstairs. To be truthful, Scrabble was always better with just her and Jodie. They had learnt to play with Mum, Dad and the Concise Oxford Dictionary. Now they had the hang of it, it was more fun to play alone. That navy blue dictionary of Dad's only held things up.

'I got something!' Jodie shouted as she came back

through the door.

'You can't have. You never even put your letters in the rack yet!'

'Nope. I mean I got something tasty – something nice from the cake shelf.'

'Not marzipan again.'

'Nope. Better than that. I got nuts. I got split almonds.'

'Won't she notice?'

'Nope. They were right at the back of the shelf. Look! Half a packet. I found 'em behind a recipe book.'

'Well,' Jenny agreed, 'if Mum lost 'em, that mean she never needed 'em.'

As they sat down to play Scrabble, Jenny tipped the almonds into the lid of the box alongside the spare letters, and placed it between them.

Jenny, of course, was the first to start.

'I got one,' she said. 'I got B-I-N – bin.' She placed the three letters in the centre of the board. Jodie stared at them.

'Let's not bother with the score,' she added.

In fact they never did add up the score when they played alone. All that extra work seemed to spoil things – like Dad's dictionary.

'What we could do,' Jenny suggested, 'is use the split almonds.'

'You lost me there.'

'Well, you git a split almond for every letter you use up.'

'That sound all right me.'

'I just won three, Jodie. B-I-N – that's three. We can eat 'em as we go along. That's your turn. Git a move on – I'm starving!'

'Let me see,' mused the younger twin. 'Let me see ... I got one! I got one! O-I-L. No, I can do better than that – B-O-I-L.'

Jodie built her word down the board, using the I from BIN. 'B-O-I-L – a boil. Okay?'

She ate four split almonds and it was Jenny's turn again.

Soon they were covering the board with words and slipping the thin, white nuts into their mouths, almost without a break. Within ten minutes the lid of the box was half-empty of letters – and completely empty of almonds.

It had not been a long game, even by their standards.

'What did you do with the packet?' Jenny asked, as she tipped the letters off the board back into the box. The last thing she wanted was their mother to find it, empty, in the bedroom. Jodie said not to worry. It was safe in her pocket and, in a moment or two, she'd take it to the kitchen bin.

'Well, you better screw it up real tight and make sure you stuff it right down to the bottom.'

But before Jodie could do so, they were surprised by the sound of tinkling bells and of people chattering outside.

Jenny was first to cross the landing. She soon stood at the window of the twin bedroom in her dressing-gown. Jodie followed shortly after her. They joined hands and –

as they had done a thousand times before – stared at the street below. Outside the Crown and Anchor, half the village seemed to be waiting in the sunshine. Rebecca Starling, with her mum and dad; the Rivers boy; the three Jackson girls; old Mrs Trinder; Simon Langley, with his mother and baby sister; Mr Maddock, the butcher ... The twins pointed excitedly and called out their names. To the left of the Crown and Anchor's porch, as seen from their window, stood a group of musicians. A violin was being tuned to the A of an accordion. As well as fiddle and squeeze-box, Jenny noticed a tin whistle.

'Look, Jodie! An orchestra!' she cried out excitedly.

No sooner did the players begin the first tune than eight or ten men, scarves on their wrists and bells on their ankles, appeared as if from nowhere and began to dance the Morris. Amongst them, Jenny spotted a tall man with red hair and beard. It was a teacher from Brayford Primary School.

'That's that Mr Leroy,' Jenny said.

'What? Over there?'

'Yip. The one with the pig's bladder blown up like a balloon and hanging from a stick. He's the clown. He's the leader. Don't you remember how he tell us about it in assembly?'

'Nope.'

'Well, he did. And if one of them dancers make just a little mistake, he have to give 'em a proper whack on the head.'

'Fancy that! Old Mr Leroy capering round like a monkey. Take all sorts, Jenny. Take all sorts, it do!'

'Yip, that take all sorts.'

'So that's what he do, weekends.'

'This isn't the weekend, Jodie. It's May Day. That's why

Dad never gone to work. That's why there's all the dancing.'

Jodie wasn't listening.

'You got burning at all?' she asked, touching her stomach again.

Jenny, who realized she had just wasted a good explanation of May Day on her sister, said her stomach *was* feeling a bit queer. But it had felt queer since Friday morning.

'Jenny! I got this awful burning. I'm going to have to lie down.'

The elder twin glanced over her shoulder in time to see Jodie leave the room. No doubt she would have followed her, but the sound of a door opening below caught her attention. Mrs Wright came out on to the pavement. As soon as a gap came in the music, she was calling across the street.

'Hello, Mr Leroy! Mr Leroy!'

The teacher, jingling at every step, came over to her side of the road. Jenny leant out of the window and saw the two heads below. For a moment she imagined Mr Leroy suddenly clonking Mum with the pig's bladder, right on the top of her skull.

'Jenny won't be in school for another week. Do you reckon you could let her teacher know? That's Mrs Rudge. But Jodie – she don't have a single spot. Fit as a fiddle, she is. I'm sending her in tomorrow.'

Mr Leroy nodded and, hardly touching the tarmac, skipped back across the road.

It was at that moment that Jenny felt a burning sensation in her stomach, too. This was followed immediately by a tightness in the throat – just below her Adam's apple – as if an invisible hand were gripping it. Even her breathing had become rapid and painful. She turned towards the room again. It seemed to be spinning.

'Jodie! Where are you, Jodie?' she called.

This was answered by a faint moan from the double bedroom. As she tottered in through the door, she saw that Jodie had collapsed across the enormous bed.

'You all right?'

It was a silly question. Jodie could not even reply. As she fell on to the mattress, she had knocked the box of Scrabble to the floor. With enormous effort Jenny bent down to tidy it up. But the sickness suddenly gripped her throat even more tightly and she slumped down on to the carpet. Her attention was caught by three small, oval shapes. Trembling, she picked one up. An almond. It was a split almond. But it did not look white or even creamy – it looked surprisingly grey. So did the second almond. The third one seemed to be more of a musty green!

'Where did you git 'em from?' she demanded.

'Git what from?' Jodie groaned.

'Almonds. Them split almonds, Jodie!'

'Kitchen.'

'But *where* in the kitchen.'

'Cupboard. I found 'em up on a shelf.'

'Behind a cookery book. You said you found 'em behind a book. Are you sure about that, Jodie? Jodie? Are you listening?'

'I'm sure. That had ... That had slipped down.'

'Oh Lord, Jodie! Where's the packet? Did you put it in the bin?'

Jodie, too sick to care, wanted only to be left alone. But her sister would give her no peace. Not till she had fumbled in her pocket and handed over the cellophane envelope.

'Oh Lord!' Jenny repeated.

'What's the matter now?'

'The *best before* date! That's what's the matter! This

packet say the nuts were best before January '76.'

Jodie gulped, then turned on the bed as if desperately reaching for air.

'Nuts don't go off ... Surely that don't!'

Jenny didn't answer. Not yet. She was trying desperately to do the awful sum. She didn't even bother to work out the months, but just counted the years. She had used every finger of her left hand. Her mouth fell open.

'Everything go off, Jodie! Everything go off with time.'

They lay on their backs and stared at the ceiling, thinking it best not to move.

'Maybe we ought to call Mum and Dad,' Jodie whimpered.

Jenny heard her, but could not decide. A fragment of almond had lodged in one of her molars. She removed it with a fingernail – yet the taste of the nut lingered on, suggesting mildew and decay.

'No point in telling 'em now,' she lamented. 'No point in making 'em angry just before ... just before we ...'

'Oh, my head's throbbing so bad,' Jodie moaned again. 'Boing! Boing! Boing! That don't let up, Jenny. Boing! Boing! Blinking boing!'

'Same with me.'

'Oh Jenny, I'm going to cry!'

'Don't you dare, Jodie,' the elder sister said. 'If you start blubbing, then I'll start too! Come on, lie down and I'll cover you up. That's it. Just you lie down.'

Both of them shivered violently in the warmth of the spring afternoon.

As Jenny arranged the blankets over her sister, another almond – like a cyanide capsule – fell to the floor. She wanted to pick it up but, suddenly sweating from the effort of moving the covers, collapsed on to the bed next to her trembling sister.

'You git in, too!' Jodie sobbed, hugging Jenny. 'You git in bed, too. Oh, Jenny! Oh Jenny! You hold me as tight as you can. We're going to go. I know it, Jenny. Oh Jenny! I can feel it. We're going!'

The elder sister had put on a brave face up to this point, but now gave in to floods of tears. As their bodies shook in despair, the twins realized the music and dancing were over. Now it was the bed itself that seemed to reel, spinning them away, away from life. Fiddle and accordion ... accordion and fiddle ... tin whistle, bells and pig's bladder – all the gaiety was eddying away. They could not hold on. They were spinning and drifting.

'Oh Jodie! Jodie! Jodie! Jodie!' Jenny wailed uncontrollably.

'Don't fret! I'm with you, Jenny. Mrs Trinder say that when her husband die, she was sure he gone to heaven. Maybe we're going to heaven too, Jenny!'

'But I don't want to go to heaven, Jodie. Not now! I don't want to go. I like it down here with Mum and Dad! I like it here in Brayford!'

They clasped each other even more firmly. The light outside was dying too. Finally, they rolled on to their backs and, as they lay there hand in hand, drifted into a dreamless sleep – deep and uninterrupted.

'Don't they look a pair!' Mrs Wright said.

Holding a breakfast tray loaded with eggs and toast, she closed the door with her bottom. Mr Wright, already bending over the bed, smiled at his daughters. He stroked their foreheads, each in turn, with his large and work-roughened hands. 'Little mites!' he muttered. 'Little mites!'

'Gentle, Eric! Wake 'em up gentle. That's best to give 'em time.'

'You'd have thought all that music and tom-foolery would have got 'em over-excited,' he said. 'The funny thing is when I come up at five o'clock last night, they were sleeping like a pair of angels.'

Neither twin had moved. Both of them still lay on their backs, eyes closed and mouths half-open.

As Mrs Wright sat on the edge, the whole mattress tilted. Mr Wright, as if in counterbalance, sat down on the other side.

A few moments later, Jenny yawned. She stretched her whole body and then sat up abruptly. She seemed puzzled. Delighted. Surprised.

'What's happening? Mum! Dad! Where am I?'

'You're in our bed!' Mr Wright laughed.

'Why? What time is it?'

'Seven o'clock,' he said.

'Morning or night!'

'Heavens, girl! That's morning,' Mrs Wright interrupted. 'You and Jodie just slept through fourteen hours.'

Jenny turned towards the other side of the bed and stared at her mother. It was good. The chinks of light that edged past the curtains were good, too. It was good just to be alive!

'You and Jodie can go back to your own room tonight,' Mrs Wright explained.

'You mean ...'

'That's right. You can sleep in your own beds. Matter of fact, you can go back now, if you like.'

'And Jodie?'

'What about her?'

'Did she ...'

'Oh no. And she won't do. Not now. Not after four

days. She's missed it this time. That's a shame, but she's as fit as a fiddle. She can get dressed and have breakfast with us. I reckon Mrs Langley or Simon will drop her off at school.'

Mr Wright said he would have to get a move on. As he stood up, the bed listed badly to starboard again. It righted itself only when Mrs Wright rose as well and walked over to draw back the curtains.

Light flooded in. Jenny noticed a last split almond – beautifully white – halfway down the counterpane. She snatched it up before her mother could turn round and clasped it in the palm of her hand.

'Mum, maybe Jodie could stay . . .'

'No, she can't. I don't want her missing her schooling. I'll do your dad's sandwiches and then we'll wake her up.'

'But, Mum, she don't look very good to me.'

'Don't you go putting silly notions in her head.'

'But, Mum!'

'No *buts* about it!'

'But . . .'

'Don't you craze me, Jenny Wright!'

'But, Mum!'

The younger twin rolled over and sat up, startling them.

She knew before they told her. Her joints ached beautifully. Her head throbbed. She felt dizzy and parched.

She was covered in spots – and smiling.

The Day-Return

'Nobody is sitting next to Gregory Stuart.'

'Sir, can we have our sandwiches now?'

'Don't be ridiculous. It's not even nine thirty. Look, there's four of you sitting at a table for six. Surely, if you didn't spread out so much, there'd be plenty of room for Gregory?'

'But we're playing cards!' Brenton Sheen explained. He was anxious to continue the game, his only regret being that they were not playing for money.

'Come on! Whose deal?' snarled Dean Fulcher, the school bully.

Mr Leroy turned to appeal to Melvyn Maddock who carried on shuffling the cards and then cut the pack.

'You can't play this game with five, Sir – honestly!' Melvyn explained. 'It's four players. Those are the rules. It's bad enough trying to play with Simon Langley, Sir. Every time it's his turn to play, he's either dozing off or staring out of the window.'

Simon – even larger than Melvyn, but blond and more sullen – shrugged off the comment and looked up at the teacher:

'Can't we just have a nibble, Sir?'

Mr Leroy shook his head. What was the point in trying? All they could think about was sandwiches and souvenirs. One thing was for sure – nobody was thinking about Gregory Stuart. A loner. He just didn't fit.

Simon was a loner, too. He lived in his own world and

159

moved at his own pace. Yet Simon Langley belonged. He belonged in Brayford. He was as much a part of the village as the Lower Green, St Peter's Church or the River Gippen.

Mr Leroy looked over to the next table where Gregory sat by himself. Gregory, who did not belong. Gregory, with his round face and round eyes; the hair that flopped, unparted, on to his forehead; the glasses that always seemed to be slipping down his nose. Like most people, Mr Leroy felt sorry for him and irritated by him at the same time.

There was always a place for loners in a village – but not for outsiders.

'How's it going, Greg?'

The boy looked up. Round face. Round eyes. Before Mr Leroy heard the reply, he knew it would be too clever by half.

'It's going at an average speed of seventy-five miles per hour, Sir.'

Typical. A typical Gregory Stuart reply. Really! You could hardly blame the others if they shunned him. Greg didn't fit. That's all there was to it. Who knows? Maybe he didn't want to fit. Whether Gregory suffered or not, what could *he* do about it? There wasn't much point in ordering the world to be kinder.

'You know what I mean, Gregory. Are you all right sitting here by yourself?'

'Fine, Sir. Any time now I'll be arriving at Chelmsford.'

Honestly! You'd have thought the boy was travelling on a different train. Nervy. Always talking of average speeds, arrival and departure times. Even now, he had a copy of *The Complete Railway Guide (Eastern Region)* on the table in front of him. That, too, was typical. So was the fact that he hadn't even taken off his coat. He clutched his packed lunch against his stomach as if they'd only just left Ipswich.

'Let the train take the strain, Sir!' Gregory suddenly added.

Ignoring this, Mr Leroy told him to take off his coat.

'But I'm not hot, Sir.'

'I don't care if you're hot or not. It's ridiculous wearing a coat on a day like this. And, for heaven's sake, put that carrier bag down. Go on. Put it down. There are plenty of spare seats.'

'I'm quite happy holding it. Can we start our lunch now, Sir?'

'No, we cannot. We haven't even got to Chelmsford yet.'

'Haven't you, Sir? I have. That was Chelmsford we just pulled out of. Would you like to look at my *Railway Guide*, Sir?'

Mr Leroy turned away and, almost before he had taken a step, bumped into Mrs Winters. She had just walked the length of the compartment handing out labels to be pinned on coats. Each was written in her neat, italic hand:

> *Brayford Primary School Party.*
> *Returning to Ipswich from Liverpool Street.*
> *17.27 hours. Platform 11.*

'There you are, Gregory,' she said. 'Pin this on your coat. If you did get lost, that's all you need to know. You just find a policeman and show him.

'I'm glad to see *someone's* taking the outing seriously,' she added, spotting Gregory's *Railway Guide*. 'Half this lot might just as well be on a trip to Timbuktu. All they seem to be interested in is comics, card games and packed lunches. If they kept their eyes open they might get something from the journey – a sense of geography, for a start. At least Gregory makes an effort.'

Gregory said, 'Thank you, Miss,' and asked if she would like a chicken leg.

The card game behind them stopped immediately and some giggles broke out.

'Would you care for a chicken leg too, Sir?'

'Gregory! How many chicken legs have you got?'

'None, Sir. I've got normal legs. But the chicken's got two.'

'You mean you brought a chicken – a whole chicken – with you?'

'Yes, Sir.'

'Does your mother always give you a whole chicken?' asked Mrs Winters.

'Only when I go on outings. Is that a spare label, Miss?'

Mrs Winters, who still held one last label in her hand, replied that it was.

'Can I have it?'

'If you want.'

She passed it to him, with a puzzled smile.

Gregory smiled too – and carefully attached the label by its safety-pin to the top of the carrier bag.

As soon as the teachers had gone, three boys were on their feet and crowding round. At last he lifted the bag from his lap, placed it on the table and hauled out a large mass wrapped in silver foil.

'That do have two legs!' Melvyn said.

Slowly Gregory unsealed the foil. A few square centimetres of dark, roasted skin were just visible. Then, without warning, he pinched the foil back in place. Behind his glasses, the round eyes glinted. He sucked in a little breath.

'That do have two legs!' he said, mimicking Melvyn.

'That have two legs – and that even have wings!'

Nothing more was said. But when the boys rejoined Simon Langley back at their table they did not even pretend to play cards. Brenton and Melvyn began sorting the packs. Simon Langley stared dreamily out of the window and Dean Fulcher pulled a war comic from his pocket. But Melvyn, the butcher's son, could not stop himself: he leant over the back of his seat and stared at the carrier bag.

'Would you like a ham sandwich?' he asked Gregory.

'I'll be all right for a bit. Nine forty-eight. In exactly one minute we should be passing Chadwell Heath.'

They did. Within the next ten minutes the Inter City 125 whisked the school party and the chicken through Seven Kings and Ilford. The landscape outside the train baffled the Suffolk children – an endless no-man's-land, neither countryside nor town. At one moment they spotted allotments, playing fields, neat rows of houses and even clumps of woodland. These gave way to old warehouses and disused factories. In the distance, blocks of grey flats sneered down at the mess below. Wider tracts of wasteland. Banks of cinder interrupted by cow parsley. Occasional hollyhocks making a last attempt at colour, though their tall stems seemed already dead. All the goods yards were full of abandoned wagons – left to rust along with their loads by drivers who'd given up hope. Closer to the line itself, rubber tyres smouldered on a bonfire, watched by a group of men in overalls.

Simon Langley, sitting next to the window, missed none of this. Most of his friends assumed he was dozing or daydreaming as usual. In fact, even though he had not rushed round with the others for a glimpse of the chicken, he *had* been listening.

He was not surprised when Sandra Thomas darted past them in Gregory's direction.

163

'Hello, Greg. What station's next, then?'

'Why do you want to know?'

'So I can put it in my Journey Writing.'

'Bethnal Green.'

'Thanks.'

'My pleasure.'

'Is that true you brought a whole chicken?'

So word had been passed back down the carriage. Gregory smiled. Whispered messages and gasps of surprise had travelled back as the train sped on.

'After Bethnal Green, it's Liverpool Street. We arrive at nine fifty-seven.'

'Are you going to eat it all by yourself?'

'Then we take the underground to Tower Bridge.'

'You're very good at maps, aren't you!'

'And at Tower Bridge, we eat our packed lunch.'

'Can I sit down here, Gregory? There's lots of empty seats.' She smiled. Her teeth were all over the place. Gregory nodded again.

In no time at all, more girls swarmed up to join them –
Wendy Stockland, Sally Warder, Rachel Conners and
Susan Webb. They were led by the girl from America.

Alabama Candy stood taller and spoke more loudly
than anyone. Her pockets were stuffed with goodies from
the American airbase where her father worked as a crew
chief.

'Say! Did your folks really roast you a chicken?'

Gregory, whose father did not live with him and his
mother, just nodded again.

'Hey! Did you see we just came through a place called
Maryland? We got a Maryland back in the States. Did you
know that, Greg? That's real cool!'

Gregory said he did know, but he thought Maryland in
the States would probably be warmer.

Alabama Candy laughed and told him he was real cool,
too. Then she glanced at the silver foil.

'Mind if I ride alongside you?' she asked.

'No. Sit down before you get your head caught in the
luggage rack.'

'Man! This cat is cool!' she declared. 'This cat is cool!'

But before she could settle down, Melvyn was leaning
over again. Dean Fulcher had elbowed his way through
the girls, followed closely by Brenton and even Simon
Langley.

Dean snarled up at Alabama Candy and told her to hop
it.

'What are you girls doing here?' shouted Melvyn. None
of them paid him any attention.

'You can't eat a whole chicken by yourself, Gregory!'
laughed Sally Warder.

The boy looked up from his *Railway Guide*, a finger
halfway down a column of place names. Round face.
Round eyes. Same smile.

'What did your mother say?' Melvyn Maddock pleaded, his face red with excitement. 'Surely she didn't just bung it in a bag! Surely your mother said something!'

'She just said to share it . . . to share it with my friends.'

'Well, then, share it with us!' Melvyn moaned. 'For heaven's sake, make a decision.'

'We're your friends,' Brenton stated.

'And I'm your friend!' Sandra insisted.

'Rubbish!' shouted Melvyn. 'Since when has she been your friend?'

Gregory's glasses had slid down his nose. He pushed them up again.

'Since Bethnal Green, I suppose.'

'I know!' said Brenton, who had ten pounds in his pocket. 'I know. You can cut it up and sell it.'

'Or we could pick cards. An ace gets a chicken leg. A king gets a wing. That's fair! That's fair!' shouted Melvyn.

'Fight you for it!' Dean Fulcher bawled, unbuttoning his coat.

Everybody stared at him till he buttoned it up again, cursing.

'I know! I got it!' Sandra said. 'We all just get our lunches out and swop 'em around a bit.'

'Swell!' Alabama Candy agreed, pulling three Hershey Bars out of her anorak.

'That might be fair,' Gregory began, 'as long as we . . .'

No one waited for the rest of the sentence.

The girls rushed back to fetch their packed lunches. The boys were already ripping theirs open. They began with sandwiches and, before long, rounds of cheese and pickle, cheese and tomato, cucumber, salmon paste, egg and cress, ham (with mustard and without), peanut butter and salami were slammed down on Gregory's table. He didn't seem particularly surprised. He was more concerned to remove the *Railway Guide* before it became stained. He had hardly done this, when the girls returned. The boys had the edge on them as far as fillings were concerned. But the girls had every variety of bread – from Sandra's baps to Sally's brown sliced, from Rachel's granary rolls to Alabama Candy's genuine Polish rye. For a moment not one of them spoke in front of the hill of food. Then Brenton threw down two almond slices. The others followed with crisps and biscuits, bars of chocolate, great slabs of cake, bananas, apples and even some grapes. Cartons of juice and cans of fizzy drink were tossed defiantly on to the pile.

'That's nothing!' said Brenton Sheen. 'If it's drink you want, I got a whole bottle of Coke. Look! Look!'

'Coke rots your teeth,' Sandra shouted.

'Well, that shouldn't bother you. You've got more gaps than teeth!' Brenton replied.

'You ought to put that bottle down quick,' Sally warned. 'You know there's a rule about glass bottles. If Mrs Winters sees it, she'll . . .'

'Why don't you mind your own business!' As he spoke, Brenton raised the Coke above Sally's reach. But Alabama Candy's hand swooped from above. She wrenched it from his grip and thrust it upward. It clonked against the rim of the luggage rack. The neck shattered. Candy stood there, aghast.

'Find the top!' Melvyn shouted. 'For Pete's sake, find the top.'

'You gotta be kidding!' wailed Alabama Candy. 'The necks busted clean off.' She stood there holding the bottle aloft – like the Statue of Liberty with her torch. But instead of spreading Freedom, she was only spreading Coke in a burst of fizzy spray that covered everyone.

As the children wiped the sticky liquid from their faces,

three adults appeared: Mrs Winters, Mr Leroy and a parent. They stared at the mountain of food on the table. It was difficult to tell where the top strata ended and the layers of sandwich began. Two rolls had cascaded to the floor like loose boulders. On the northern slopes a gentle trickle of Coke zig-zagged down the crevices.

Mr Leroy oddly enough, seemed quite calm in a crisis. He asked Mrs Winters to fetch one of the large black bags packed for unpleasant emergencies.

'You were told not to eat on the train,' he said, 'and you were told about glass bottles. Well, it's your fault. It's all your own fault . . .'

Before the children's eyes, he leant over and, like a Titan shaping the face of the earth, swept the food-mountain in-to the sack.

'Couldn't we have saved the sandwiches, Sir?' Melvyn asked sheepishly.

'No, we could not. It would only need one splinter of glass. You may be silly enough to take the risk, but I am not. We're meant to be visiting the Tower of London, not St Thomas' Hospital!'

'Never mind,' Brenton said. 'We've still got the chicken.'

'Not any more, you haven't!' the teacher declared. 'I'm sorry, Gregory. But if you'd brought a sensible packed lunch, none of this would have happened. I'll take care of that blessed chicken.'

'Yes, Sir, but . . .'

'But what?'

'I did want Mrs Winters to have a drumstick. It's already arranged.'

'Very funny. Now, all of you, back to your seats, please. And make sure you're wearing your labels. London's a very big city.'

Silent, obedient, the children checked their labels. They had gone too far and they knew it. Returning to his place, Simon Langley realized that Brenton had palled up with John Speirs. That left him without a partner. He glanced back at Gregory who still sat alone, realizing they had something in common.

'I can't believe it!' Mr Leroy muttered. 'We haven't even got to London yet, and this has to happen.'

Gregory looked up at the teacher. Round face. Round eyes. Suddenly they were in a different, clearer light as the train slid under the vast glass roof of Liverpool Street Station.

'We've just pulled in, Sir. Nine fifty-seven. Bang on time, as it happens.'

Two stops on the Circle Line and they had arrived at Tower Hill. It was all quite carefully planned. There were toilets near by and benches where they could sit down for

169

a light snack. Simon Langley told Gregory not to give up hope about the chicken and passed him a banana that had survived the riot. It was best not to push your luck with Leroy. Best to wait till after the river trip. Anyway, a roast chicken would hardly have been a snack. Gregory smiled and ate the banana as Simon sketched the view of Tower Bridge.

Before they knew it, it was ten fifty-five and the entire party had settled down on board the pleasure boat *Witheycombe*. Gregory had somehow obtained a leaflet and was checking the times of sailing. He nodded approvingly as their boat swung out into the tide and nosed her way past the long, grey destroyer, *HMS Belfast*. Schoolchildren in red, yellow and blue clambered amongst her guns like some lunatic crew sworn to the service of mischief.

'To make your journey a little more instructive,' said the cockney commentator, 'I shall be pleased to offer you a guide to the historic sights that fall beneath your eyes. I would stress that this service is entirely voluntary. You may show your appreciation, if you so wish, by placing a gratuity in the captain's hat. This will be held forth, in the traditional manner, as you alight at Westminster ...'

'Say! This guy is way-out!' Alabama shouted with delight. 'What the heck is *alight* supposed to mean? Man, are we going to *alight*?'

'*Alight* means "get off",' Mr Leroy explained.

'Alight my foot or I'll thump you! Could you say that?' growled Dean Fulcher.

Nobody paid him any attention. Mrs Winters explained that *alight* was just a polite word. That was all. Mr Leroy laughed.

'Actually,' he added, 'we don't alight at Westminster. Did you hear that, everybody? Nobody gets off this boat

170

at Westminster. Are you listening? You don't even leave your seats. This boat will take us back to Tower Pier.'

'Excuse me, Sir,' Gregory interrupted. He had run his finger down a list of sailing times. 'Excuse me, but . . .'

'No, Gregory. You cannot have your chicken back. Not yet. When we have lunch at the Tower of London, I might think about it.'

Gregory shrugged. Same face. Same smile.

'To the starboard, that is the left side of our vessel, you may see *HMS Belfast* – a destroyer that saw notable service in 1943, playing no mean part in the sinking of the German battleship, *Scharnhorst*.'

Gregory jotted down the name and date. Simon Langley, sketching with meticulous care, worked too slowly to capture the sights around them. *Witheycombe*, like life itself, bore him along too fast. Before long they reached their destination.

Westminster. The seat of government.

It was a disaster.

The commentator, tipping coins from the captain's hat into a money bag, now spoke with cockney bluntness. In fact, he was giving the teacher, Mr Leroy, a piece of his mind.

'You can sit on this boat if you want, mate, but I'm telling yer, we don't sail back to Tower Pier for an hour an' a quarter. You deaf or somefing? If you gone and booked your lot in for a return trip, that's your lookout. This is a boat, my son, not a blinkin' taxi-cab . . . Well, if that's what they told yer, then they didn't ought to, did 'ey! Don't tell me, mate! You tell the bloke who runs the booking office. Meanwhile, you get off this boat and you get on that one – *The Faery Queen*. Eight minutes. No hard feelings, son, but I'm entitled to a lunchbreak!'

The real problem was not the boats – it was

Westminster Pier. At least sixty American tourists – all as tall and healthy as Candy – were crowding the quay, ready to board *The Faery Queen*. They were students from the University of Ohio. It wasn't worth arguing about that because they all wore sweatshirts to prove it.

'Holy smoke! Am I glad we alight!' bawled Candy. Already she was hollering greetings to the students as if they came from the same village.

'Keep together!' the teachers ordered. 'Don't rush, now. Stay with your partners.'

The crush of people was so great, there was hardly room for bags and rucksacks between all the bodies. The Ohio students seemed not to care. Everywhere, suntanned giants were grouping up for photos – whistling, laughing, shouting invitations. Alabama Candy leapt for joy and even had her picture taken. One tourist swung his camera round, catching Mrs Ratchett on the shoulder with a foot of zoom lens. 'That really riled me!' she commented later. 'But what could you do at the time?'

There was no point in even trying to count the children. Mrs Winters managed to lead an advance British platoon to the deck of *The Faery Queen*. Others followed, one or two even scrambling through the legs of the Americans. Sandra, meanwhile, was pulling at Mr Leroy's jacket and asking if there was still time to buy an ice-cream. Some were shouting, 'Save us a place!' Gregory waited near the back. Same eyes. Same smile. Even Simon hurried forward, leaving his partner behind. How they did it, nobody knew. But they had boarded safely, along with sixty Americans. The chain was hooked back across the deck railings.

'Welcome aboard *The Faery Queen*,' came the voice through the microphone. 'In order to render your journey more interesting, it is my pleasure to draw your attention to the many historical monuments we shall be passing. This commentary is entirely voluntary. Should you wish to offer a gratuity, the captain's hat will be ...'

'Oh no! Where's Gregory Stuart?' gasped Mrs Winters.

Mr Leroy looked at her. He turned white. He could not speak.

'I'm here, Sir,' came a small voice from behind the teachers.

'Thank heaven for that. I thought, for a moment, we'd left one of the party on Westminster Pier.'

'We did, Sir.'

'Sorry?'

'Look for yourself, Sir.'

Everyone in earshot spun round to stare at the quay. It was empty apart from two figures: a Japanese gentleman in a neat blue blazer and a lady – presumably his wife – in a matching blue suit.

The lady was holding a carrier bag. She peered inside it as if half-expecting to find a bomb. She seemed quite relieved to find nothing but a foil-wrapped chicken.

Mr Leroy, of course, said he was sorry. But all afternoon he thought of the chicken. How many times had he said to his class that saying sorry was a bit too easy! As he ate his own lunch he felt even worse. The children were very good about it. He remembered the soaked mess he'd pushed into the rubbish bag. Maybe he'd had to clear the table fast. But the loss of a whole chicken was quite another story.

'I shouldn't worry too much,' said Mrs Ratchett – a dinner lady at Brayford School as well as a parent. 'What I'd like to know is, how do Mrs Stuart afford to send him with a whole chicken anyway. I mean, he have free dinners. If she can't afford his school meal, how do she afford a chicken? Tax-payers' money, that is. People want something for nothing, they do. They do, these days.'

This did not make Mr Leroy feel much better.

'His mother did say the chicken was to be shared,' Mrs Winters commented.

Mr Leroy felt even worse.

'Yes, but in a way, that's you and me pay for it in the first place.'

The afternoon was too hot for argument. It was ten past four. Two teachers and four parents sat down on a bench by Traitor's Gate. Very appropriate, Mr Leroy thought. All around them tired, hungry but contented children clutched their clipboards. Sketches and notes were held up for approval – the Crown Jewels, the Block, swords, pistols, cannons and battlements. 'Like this, Miss?' 'Like my picture of Big Harry's armour, Sir?'

Simon Langley's sketches were particularly good. They had spent several hours at the Tower.

Even Gregory Stuart came up. He had jotted down a list of one hundred dates.

'Very good, Gregory. But what will you do with them?'

Same face. Same smile . . .

'Not sure, Sir. I'll think of something.' Already a complex system of arrows had been scrawled all over his paper.

'I am sorry, Gregory.'

'That's all right, Sir. I'll write it out neatly back at home.'

'No. I'm sorry about the chicken.'

'Not as sorry as Mrs Winters!'

'But it wasn't her fault.'

'I know.'

'So?'

'So she'll be extra sorry not to get her drumstick.'

174

'Oh, Gregory!' sighed Mrs Winters. 'You're the one who's missed out. You must have been dying to eat your chicken!'

He pushed his glasses back up his nose.

'Not really, Miss.'

'What do you mean?'

'Well, I'm going off meat, Miss – especially chicken. I thought I might become a vegetarian.'

'Boys of your age do not become vegetarians!' snapped Mrs Ratchett.

'No. But they might want to sometimes,' Mrs Winters commented gently.

'Why didn't you tell your mum, if you really don't like chicken?'

'I do like chicken, Sir. That's why I don't like eating them.'

'Right,' Mr Leroy said. 'I'll try again. Why didn't you tell your mother you did not want to bring a roast chicken to eat on this school outing?'

'But I did, Sir.'

'What did she say?'

'She said it was too late. It was roasted and wrapped. She said to eat the rolls and fruit and, if I was still a vegetarian by lunchtime, to share the chicken out among my friends.'

Rush hour at Liverpool Street was nearly as bad as the pier. But by now everybody had learnt their lesson. The Brayford children kept together. To be lost in this welter of people would be nothing less than terrifying. People. Grey-faced, haggard, sweating. They swarmed out of tubes and in from the streets, from cafeterias and booking offices – all towards the platforms. They humped their bodies, like so much baggage, into the waiting trains. At the back of the party, Simon Langley walked with Gregory. He suddenly realized that they had become partners again. Different, but together. Gregory realized this, too.

'What runs from London to Ipswich,' he asked, 'and arrives without leaving the station?'

Simon shrugged.

'A railway line,' Gregory said, smiling.

Simon would need to think about that one. They both stepped into the train.

Almost as soon as they were seated in the reserved carriage, Alabama Candy screamed.

'Oh, brother! This cannot be true. Somebody tell me I'm dreaming.'

Two oriental faces were peering through her window. She fell back on to her seat, her eyes screwed tight, her fists pounding the table.

'Man! This is gonna blow my mind!'

Rachel Conners pushed past her and pulled open the small top window.

'Gregory!' she called.

Gregory arrived, Mr Leroy close behind him.

The Japanese gentleman and wife stood there, polite and calm. He was holding up a white carrier bag and his wife was pointing to the label.

Brayford Primary School Party.
Returning to Ipswich from Liverpool Street.
17.27 hours. Platform 11.

'Thank you! Thank you!' Gregory called.

'This is our pleasure,' the gentleman said. For a moment he looked as if he were going to bow – but he pushed the chicken through the window instead.

Five twenty-six. Five twenty-seven. When the train left, everyone was cheering. But oddly enough, Gregory had just plonked the chicken down on the table.

After Bethnal Green the bonfire of tyres was still smouldering. Gregory drew a few more arrows on his list of dates. But soon his pencil slipped out of his hand and his head lay against his arms on the table, next to the chicken. Maybe somebody would have woken him up. But somehow the idea of cutting up the chicken, of buying or bartering or betting for the pieces, seemed unthinkable – even to Dean. Mrs Winters, too, said not to wake him. Best not to wake him. She rolled up his coat and placed it beneath his head. The head turned. The lips pouted. He reminded her of a small child.

'Look at him! Just look at him!' Mrs Ratchett said – and by now even she was whispering. 'When he's asleep he look like a babe, he do. He could be in another world.'

'Gregory's in another world when he's awake,' Mr Leroy thought. But he said nothing.

Chelmsford, Colchester, Manningtree. They crossed the Stour estuary where a flock of oystercatchers stalked the mudflats, stabbing. They were back in Suffolk. It was low tide.

Waiting on the platform, parents listened for the train. At last it came through the final cut, round the last bend and into the station.

Sandra Thomas was out first and in her mother's arms. Sally and Rachel followed; then a group of boys. Mothers jostled down the platform, wide-eyed as if they had never quite expected to see their children again.

Clunk ... Clunk. Clunk. Doors slammed. Apart from the hugs and 'thank you for taking them' and even a few brushed-away tears, the journey was done.

Simon stood by his father, showing him his sketches.

177

Gregory's mother hugged the breath from his body. He had hardly rubbed the sleep from his eyes.

'Did you go to Westminster?'

'Yes. On the *Witheycombe*.'

'And the Tower? Did you like the Tower?'

'Yes. It was great.'

Clunk.

The last door was shut and the train moved off.

'You're a good boy. And did you share the chicken?'

'Oh! Oh, Mum ...' Gregory faltered.

Simon Langley stopped dead and spun round to look back at his friend.

Mr Leroy had heard the mother's question too. His mouth fell open.

'Yes, Mum. We saw ... the Tower of London.'

'The chicken's all gone!' Simon Langley shouted. 'It was tremendous, Mrs Stuart. And it's gone!'

'That's what I like to hear!' she answered, planting another wet kiss on her boy's cheek.

Afterwards Gregory looked over to the teachers, then back to his partner, Simon.

Round face. Round eyes.

'That's gone all right,' he said.

At seven thirty-two, undisturbed on the table, the chicken arrived at Norwich Station.

The Leavers' Service

That was it, really.

Once the Leavers' service was over, that was it. Gregory's teacher, Mr Leroy, felt pleased on the whole. They could relax now. There was only Friday to go. A few irritations to be coped with maybe. A lost library book to find. An art cupboard to be cleared out. But that was peanuts. The fourth-year leavers were already packed up. Autograph books were signed. One or two of the girls had looked quite weepy when the speech had been made and the mugs, marked Brayford Primary School, had been handed out. By and large the service had gone very well.

Gregory's watch, of course, had been a fly in the ointment. But that was Gregory all over. It was best to play it down. After all, Gregory wasn't going to lose any sleep over it. So why should he, the class teacher? The business about the mug had been awkward too. But the governors had gone now. So had Mr Fletcher, the visiting speaker from the Education Office. You'd have thought the headteacher would let the matter rest. Odd that he had asked Mr Leroy to his office. Still, if he wanted a post-mortem . . .

Mr Leroy was even more surprised to find Mr Gibson's office full of people. Mr Gibson himself sat behind his desk. Gregory's mother, Mrs Stuart, sat on the edge of an easy chair, several feet below him. Even the deputy head, Mrs Rudge, had been called in. She looked rather hot and tired. Her face, next to that of Mrs Stuart, seemed very long.

'Ah ... Do sit down, Mr Leroy,' said the head. 'We've just asked Mrs Stuart to pop in so we can say our goodbyes.'

'And I wanted to thank you,' said the mother, 'for doing your best by Gregory.'

'Doing my best by Gregory,' the teacher thought. 'That's a funny way of putting it.' A year with Gregory and he was still a total mystery. His math's book looked like a set of secret codes recorded upside down in mirror writing. Yet Gregory had scored the highest marks of all when the fourth year did the county test in February. Same with everything. If there was a way to get the right answer with the wrong method, Gregory would find it. Often there seemed to be no method at all in his inventions. A loner. An enigma. Mr Leroy was not sure if he would be glad to see him go or miss him.

He sat down uncomfortably on the easy chair between Mrs Stuart and the deputy.

Gregory, his back to the wall, smiled down at them. His glasses slipped down his nose so that he had to push them up again.

Suddenly Mr Leroy understood. He understood why three teachers had come together to meet mother and son. This was the teachers' last chance. Not that they wanted to punish Gregory. It was nothing like that. But all of them wanted to know. Had he planned the whole thing? Did he know what he was doing? Was he an oddball by nature – or was it by design? Today, for instance – in the Leavers' service. When he reached forward to shake hands with the education officer and his digital watch had blipped out a tune, was all that part of a plan? If not, it was an incredible coincidence; if it was, it was brilliantly timed. Obviously Gregory could not have known that Mr Fletcher would be so startled. No one expected him to drop the mug. Not that you could blame him.

'Surely, Gregory,' Mrs Rudge began, 'surely it would have been more sensible not to wear your watch at all if it's the blipping kind.'

'Yes, Miss.'

'Well, then, why did you wear it?'

'I do like to keep an eye on the time, Miss.'

It was hard to believe a smile could be so intelligent and so innocent.

'And how long have you had your watch, Gregory?'

'Which watch, Miss?' he replied.

'Don't be silly! The watch you're wearing ...'

Gregory lifted his arms slightly. As the sleeves of his sweater rose, the three teachers realized that there was in fact a watch on each wrist.

'But, Gregory!' exclaimed the headteacher. 'You can't wear two watches at the same time. That's completely crazy!'

'No, it's not, Sir.' Same smile, as he pushed his glasses up his nose again. 'One of them isn't working.'

Mrs Stuart nodded, as if her boy had a point there. The three teachers exchanged glances. Was she in this, too?

'He's right, you know,' she explained. 'The one on his left wrist stopped way back in February.'

'Then why's he wearing two watches now?'

'His grandad – that's muh father – come doon fro' Glasgow and he give muh boy the money to buy a brand new one. Fifteen poons. He chose one that'll give 'ee a tune as well as the tame o' day.'

Mr Gibson stared at her as if she had gone mad. Why was she suddenly talking in a broad Scottish accent? Was she as mischievous as her son?

Mr Leroy noticed the accent too, but knew it was no sham. Ever since her father had come down to join them in Brayford, four weeks ago, she had begun to slip back into the speech of her family and childhood. 'Tame', she'd say, instead of 'time'. The schoolchildren were 'the bairns'; infants were 'wee and bonny'. Even Gregory's speech had occasional traces of Scottish. Once or twice, 'I didn't know' had popped out as 'I didna ken'.

'I thought your father just came down for Christmas,' said Mr Gibson. He could still remember the white-haired Scot who'd burst in on the Christmas party and made such an impression on the younger children. The Starling girl had even spread a rumour that he was the real Santa Claus. The Wright twins and several others were convinced in the end. (Why Father Christmas should be related to Gregory Stuart and why he travelled around Brayford in a taxi cab, remained a mystery to them.)

'So he came down for Christmas, then went back to Glasgow ...'

'Aye an' in June he come doon agin. Only this tame, he's come doon to stay. A hoos here in Brayford. I'll no' complain, Mr Gibson. I'll no' complain.

The headteacher glanced at the boy's record card. In six years he'd been to five different schools, each in a different town.

'We're all very pleased for you, Mrs Stuart. We hope you'll be very happy here. As for the watch – the one that *is* working ...'

'I'm sorry about that,' Gregory said. 'Is it all right if I put my arms down now, Sir?'

'Yes, of course.'

Mr Leroy – a day from the end of term – could not take it too seriously. His mind went back an hour to the Leavers' service. The education officer had made quite a nice little speech. Usual sort of thing. 'Wherever you go, remember that you represent your school – and what a

182

fine school it is. Some of you may be nervous about your new life ahead. That's quite natural. We're all a little frightened when we begin something new. Above all, you must look on it as an adventure – an opportunity . . .' And then the first line of leavers had stood up and Mrs Rudge led them to the edge of the stage. She pushed Sandra Thomas up the steps. The others followed, one by one. Then she prepared the second line, adjusting Dean Fulcher's tie and insisting he swallow his chewing-gum. First row back, second row up; second row back, third row up . . . Mr Fletcher, despite the rather fierce look his horn-rimmed glasses gave him, spoke softly and kindly to every leaver, shaking hands and handing each their mug. No delay. No hitch. As smooth as clockwork. Well, as smooth as silicon chips, you might say.

Gregory, of course, was in the third row, standing right at the end. His blue sweater was a size too large, but apart from that, he looked quite smart. Five mugs left on the table. Four. Three. Two. Then just one. Gregory walked across the stage. He had not forgotten, but raised his right arm in order to shake hands. Mr Fletcher smiled down at the last of the leavers . . . and that's when it happened, to the tune of *Oh, Tannenbaum*.

beep beepy-beep
beep beepy-beep
beep beepy-beep
beep beepy-beep

The digital alarm startled two hundred parents, teachers and children. A Christmas carol, for heaven's sake! A Christmas carol, right in the middle of July.

Mr Fletcher dropped the mug. It shattered. In the silence, the watch repeated its tune. Trying to smile, Mr Fletcher leant forward and said a few words to Gregory. Pushing his glasses back up his nose, the boy left the stage and returned to his line. *Oh, Tannenbaum, Oh, Tannenbaum* still echoing in their ears, the school stood up and sang *Jerusalem*.

Mr Leroy would never forget that. Sitting on the easy chair in the head's office, he smothered a chuckle and tried to concentrate on Gregory's interrogation. Mrs Rudge was trying very hard to keep calm.

'So you knew your watch – the new watch that your grandfather bought you in June – you knew it had an alarm!'

'Yes.'

'And you must have known how to turn it off.'

'No.'

'Well, let me put it another way. You must have known how to turn it on.'

'No.'

'So you're trying to tell me that your watch has been playing *Oh, Tannenbaum, Oh, Tannenbaum* at two

184

thirty-five precisely every day for the last four weeks?'

'No.'

'Well, for heaven's sake, explain!'

'Every day at two thirty-five precisely for the last *three* weeks,' he corrected her. 'Grandad gave me the watch right at the end of June.'

'Gregory,' the headteacher interrupted. 'Are you ... Do you ... Are you doing this on purpose?'

'Doing what on purpose, Sir?'

'Never mind.'

'But I do mind, Sir.'

'Never mind, I said. Mr Leroy, do you have any questions you would like to raise?'

Mr Leroy, who had been trying to remember whether Gregory's score on the last test had been 136 or 137, jolted. He recovered himself.

'Gregory,' he asked. 'When you went into the service, you must surely have known that your watch had an alarm function?'

The headmaster smiled. He liked this. Mr Leroy could handle technicalities, even in a crisis. He would go far.

'Yes, Sir,' Gregory said.

'Then you knew it was set to play.'

'No, Sir.'

'Why not?'

'I thought I had turned the fifth function off, Sir. But I couldn't be certain.'

'Why couldn't you be certain, Gregory?'

'Because of the instructions.'

'Hold on. You are now saying that you didn't know how to turn off the alarm function because of the instructions?'

'No, Sir. I mean yes, you're right.'

'Surely the instructions told you ...'

'They didn't tell me anything.'

'Why not. Surely a boy of your ability ...'

'They're written in Japanese, Sir.'

Mr Gibson, thinking no doubt of the holiday ahead, interrupted again and said it was time to be going. He thanked Mrs Rudge and Mr Leroy for their trouble. They left with Gregory to return to their classrooms.

'Mrs Stuart,' said the headmaster, when they found themselves alone, 'there's no doubt about it, your son is what we call a lateral thinker.'

'Aye,' she said. 'And what does that mean?'

'It means he thinks sideways as well as forwards.'

Mrs Stuart was not sure whether to apologize or be pleased.

'His IQ is well above one-hundred-and-thirty-five. That's very high, you know.'

'IQ?'

'Intelligence.'

He made it sound like a high temperature.

'No point in fretting,' she said quietly. 'It'll surely come doon wi' tame.'

Mr Leroy had worked with Gregory for a year. He wasn't going to give up the struggle, just at the end.

As the last child left the class at three forty-five on the very last day, he went to the door and called Gregory back.

'There's still one thing I don't understand,' he said. 'Why of all things did your watch play *Oh, Tannenbaum, Oh, Tannenbaum*?'

'I don't know,' said the boy. 'Who's Tannenbaum, anyway?'

'*Oh, Tannenbaum* is the name of the tune.'

'Is that Japanese too, Sir.'

'No, Gregory. It's German. It's German for Christmas tree. Not very seasonal for July!'

'That's what the man who made the speech said.'

'Can I have a look at your digital watch, Gregory?'

The boy passed it to him and Mr Leroy began to press a few buttons.

'We were all very sorry about the presentation mug. I've asked the secretary, but there aren't any spares. It does seem a bit of a shame.'

'Not really, Sir.'

'What do you mean?'

'Well, my grandad's bought a house right by the school. So you could say I'm not really leaving. Number 3 Drakesmere. Look for yourself, Sir.'

The teacher couldn't believe it. He peered through the classroom window. Almost directly opposite, he saw a figure with white beard and hair, wearing a red sweater and jeans. The Scotsman did not notice them but continued digging his vegetable patch.

Suddenly a new tune blipped out. It was *Auld Lang Syne*.

'That's very good, Sir. How did you do it?'

'Oh, I don't know, Gregory. But really, *Auld Lang Syne* would have been much better.'

'Thanks for finding that function, Sir.'

'Gregory – it's time you went home.'

THE DOOR IN THE AIR AND OTHER STORIES

Margaret Mahy

A varied and unusual collection of thought-provoking short stories full of fantasy and magic for the young teenager. An exciting departure for Margaret Mahy, demonstrating her astonishing range.

TEN IN A BED

Allan Ahlberg

An energetic and witty collection of stories about Dinah Price and the surprising visitors she has to entertain. Each night she finds a different fairy tale character occupying her bed – from Puss in Boots and Sleeping Beauty to a wicked witch and a wolf! They all refuse to budge until Dinah has told them a special bedtime story.

PAST EIGHT O'CLOCK

Joan Aiken

An enchanting collection of stories which are all concerned with sleeping and waking, dreams and bedtime. Each of the eight stories is woven around the theme of a familiar lullaby or bedtime song. Illustrated by the inimitable Jan Pienkowski.

PARK'S QUEST
Katherine Paterson

When Park visits his dad's father's family he discovers many things which his mother had failed to reveal to him. It comes as a surprise to discover that his Uncle Frank is married to a Vietnamese woman who has a daughter called Thanh. Then Park sees a photograph of Thanh's mother with an American airman, and things begin to fall into place . . .

BAGTHORPES LIBERATED
Helen Cresswell

In the seventh book about the eccentric Bagthorpe family, Mrs Bagthorpe is determined to liberate the female members of the household from domestic drudgery, and sets out to rally support for her radical views. But a string of hilarious incidents proves all too clearly that if there is one thing Mrs Bagthorpe can never be, it's liberated.

ME, JILL ROBINSON AND THE CHRISTMAS PANTO
Anne Digby

Jill and her family move from London to a new town – new house, new school, new friends. Jill soon becomes best friends with Lindy Hill, the madcap daughter of the town's mayor. Sarah meets the youth club leader, Roy Brewster, and the youth club quickly becomes the centre of the family's activities.

THE BURNING QUESTIONS OF
BINGO BROWN
Betsy Byars

Has there ever been a successful writer named Bingo? Has there ever been a successful person with freckles? These are just some of the burning questions in Bingo Brown's life – but where is he going to find the answers? When his worst enemy moves in next door and Bingo keeps falling in love, he knows the question marks are getting larger. But with The Most Thrilling Day and The Worst News of his life still to come, Bingo finds he has a long way to go!

PRINCESS FLORIZELLA
Philippa Gregory

Poor Princess Florizella! She really isn't like other princesses at all. She isn't beautiful. She wants to share her palace with people who don't have homes. She loves eating huge meals, and she refuses to be rescued by a handsome prince, and never wants to marry anyone. But unfortunately her parents, a very ordinary King and Queen, have other ideas in mind.

MAGGIE AND ME
Ted Staunton

Maggie is the undisputed Greenapple Street Genius. She's always got some brilliant plan – and Cyril inevitably has to help her. Whether it's getting back at the school bully or swapping places for piano lessons, these best friends are forever having adventures. Poor Cyril! Life without Maggie would be an awful lot easier, but then it would be much more boring. What would he do if she ever moved away? Ten stories about the intrepid duo.